Secret Lady

by

Beth Trissel

Ladies in Time, Book 3

Secret Lady

Cover Art by *Debbie Taylor*

The Wild Rose Press, Inc.
PO Box 708
Adams Basin, NY 14410-0708
Visit us at www.thewildrosepress.com

Publishing History
First Fantasy Rose Edition, 2019
Print ISBN 978-1-5092-2391-6
Digital ISBN 978-1-5092-2392-3

Ladies in Time, Book 3
Published in the United States of America

She took a steadying breath, turned the brass knob, and stepped into the room. The fragrance of lavender greeted her. Grandma G. had tucked sachets under her mattress to help her sleep and left small cloth bags in the drawers of an antique dresser. A sachet of apricot scented agrimony lay beneath her pillow.

This age-old herb was thought to induce slumber and offer protection against the dark forces. Other powerful herbs scented the room. Angelica, St. John's Wort, and sage were in the bunch on the bedside stand beside the antique brass lamp with an ornamental white shade.

The walk-in, but duck your head, closet at the far side of the room summoned her. Boxes of Christmas decorations, a Santa, and reindeer figures stored inside the slanted nook partially hid the steps leading to the attic and the presence she swore was there. She hadn't encountered the being in question. Yet. It wasn't cool for a nineteen-year-old to harbor terrors of a closet, but she did.

She threw her hands up after a particularly loud summons. "What do you want from me?"

There was a rap on the downstairs door.

Dedication

To my dear brother Chad,
who supported my writing in his own quiet way
and whose gentle presence is greatly missed.
See you on the other side, Brother.

Chapter One

*June, Present Day, the Shenandoah Valley of
Virginia, Victorian Farmhouse on the Lavender and
Lace Herb Farm*

The closet. It had always been about the closet, and
Evie McIntyre strove to delay the nightly trek to her
room.

Still wearing the Victorian styled gown Grandma
G. had decreed for helping in the herb shop or giving
garden tours, Evie hugged the tufted mauve couch,
darting uneasy glances at the doorway. Mounds of
violet sprigged cloth overflowed the velvet upholstery,
nearly engulfing the cat. She wasn't exactly comfy in a
full skirt and corset better suited to *Gone with the Wind*,
but changing clothes meant going upstairs.

Chimes. The ornately carved, hand painted mantel
clock struck eleven. She tensed, inhaling the voluptuous
sweetness of the peachy pink roses in the etched crystal
vase by the clock.

Maybe Grandma G. wouldn't notice her parked in
the parlor this evening?

Yeah, right.

Sure enough, the indomitable Gladys McIntyre
padded into the room on the last chime. Ever elegant,
she'd changed from her Victorian dress into a frilly
lilac robe and satin slippers. The light from a stained-

glass lamp played over her long silver hair.

She surveyed Evie and the purring gray tabby at her side, her ample chest heaving in an impatient sigh. "Figured you'd be down here with Tiddles."

Evie met her grandmother's narrowed gaze, the same blue-gray hue as her own, staring back at her with weary annoyance. "He has too much sense to go upstairs."

"For heaven's sake. This isn't a bedchamber." Puffing in exasperation, Grandma G. swept her dimpled hand at the frilly room, papered in tiny bunches of lavender, and decorated much as it might have been a century or more ago. The decor was frou-frou feminine, but many of their visitors were female, and the strong-minded widow did as she liked.

The random collection of several lifetimes crammed a large glass cabinet, spilling out onto tables and book shelves. A porcelain Jack and Jill skipped up the hill beside figurines dressed for a ball. Petal-filled jars of potpourri wafted a spicy floral scent. Vintage valentines and beribboned chocolate boxes covered in anything from hearts to flowers, to oddly enough kittens, kept company with framed photos from bygone days.

All very charming, Evie supposed, except for the presence she sensed upstairs. Visitors didn't stay long enough for that shudder-worthy experience. A braver soul would march up there, swing open the closet door, and face whatever summoned her. But Evie didn't feel particularly courageous, quite the opposite, actually.

Another huff escaped her grandmother. "Evelyn Louise, you cannot camp on the couch like some passerby caught in a snowstorm." She waved at her.

"Wearing that."

"It's my favorite," Evie lied.

"It'll wrinkle." Grandma G. was nuts about these historic costumes.

"I have six more. Plus." Evie's Victorian wardrobe reflected her grandmother's preference for fashions of the past.

"Don't be ridiculous. That's not night attire." Grandma G. paused, her plump face creased in thoughtful lines. "Besides, *the whispers* never hurt anyone…much."

Evie startled. "What?" There was something the secretive woman wasn't telling her.

"Nothing." Grandma G. waved her off like a buzzing fly. "I haven't even heard them lately."

She didn't hear anything as well as she used to, and Evie almost envied her. "I have," she muttered. "The creep factor's enough to make me go Goth, and the Victorian era suits the darkling fashion perfectly."

Her grandmother rolled her eyes. "No. It doesn't." She stepped further into the room. "When did you last hear them?"

"Now. They're louder than usual." Even admitting that out loud made Evie want to squirm.

"Really?" Grandma G. sank into a fat flouncy chair patterned in pink roses. Gray brows drawn together, she tilted her head, cupping a hand behind her ear. "The only sound I detect is that hoot owl in the oak tree outside the window."

"They're indistinct, like the fragments captured on the Electronic Voice Recorders," Evie clarified, reciting an explanation from the supernatural based TV shows she'd seen. "And my room is the worst for *the whispers*, especially the closet. Maybe it holds some dark mystery and the local ghost hunters could help. They've asked to come. More than once."

A derisive snort intruded on her suggestion, and Grandma G. shook her head. "I am not having that paranormal bunch setting up their equipment in here and staying the night. All we need are people saying the house is haunted."

"They already do, Grandma. Hasn't hurt business any."

She shrugged. "Even so, we don't want to invite more gossip. We're a happy place folk want to visit, have tea parties, and hold weddings. Not conduct séances or ghost tours."

"True. But if the house is trying to tell us something, the paranormal society might help us figure it out."

"Not my kind of *society,* girl. The house will just have to tell us what it wants. Likely *you*, as you're picking up the chatter." The older woman gave a short laugh. "Hear that, House? Tell this young thing what you want. I'm going to bed. You best head up soon, Evie."

Her stomach tightened. "I will." *Just not right now.*

"Leave as many lamps on as you want, but don't light any more candles. Might burn the place down next thing."

"Sorry about the rug." Evie smothered a small fire on her nightstand with the Oriental carpet beside her bed, and it had to be replaced.

"Lay off the matches. And remember, loads of folk will turn up tomorrow with lavender at its peak. I'll need all hands on deck." Grandma G. patted her chest above her heart, offering a smile to ease the tension. "I have a few miles left in me yet, and there's a place for you here. You'll see."

God forbid. Evie didn't want to disappoint her, but she could hardly bear to stay the summer as she'd promised, let alone indefinitely.

"Don't make me wait until your brothers are old enough to help," her grandmother coaxed.

"Alene?" Evie attempted, naming her younger seventeen-year-old sister.

"I can't have that purple haired tattooed girl assisting guests, even if she agreed to get on board. Besides, you're suited to Lavender House. It likes you."

"What?" Was her grandmother giving the home emotions now? What next?

"No need to look at me bug-eyed. I only meant you belong here. Think on my offer." She heaved herself to her feet.

"I will," Evie promised, with no such intention.

This might have to be a career option for the foreseeable future, though. College was currently a bust. No scholarships for a solid C student, and her parents weren't exactly loaded. Plus, she didn't have a clue what she wanted to do except not go into *that room*.

The shrewd woman considered her. "You want to know about the house? Begin by learning more of its history. For starters, this nineteenth structure was built over a log cabin that dates to the seventeen hundreds."

"That old?"

"Sure is. And it's been through a number of hands, including a Mennonite family named Wenger. They built most of what stands now and rebuilt after *The*

Burning." Grandma G. pursed her lips. "You know, in eighteen sixty-four when Sheridan and the Union Army torched their way through the Shenandoah Valley during the Civil War?"

Evie bent forward, trying to remember what she'd learned in school, or from her history buff father. "Was this house affected?"

"Badly damaged, and the barn was destroyed, along with other outbuildings, the harvested corn, wheat, and hay crops. The Wenger family lost everything."

Disbelief swept over her. "But Mennonites are good peaceful people."

Grandma G. glanced away with a frown. "Their goodness made no difference to Sheridan. Or their pacifism. He granted few exceptions. Mennonites suffered along with everyone else."

"Why haven't I heard any of this before?"

"You have. I'm not going into all of it again now. Besides, your father told you plenty, if you think back." Smothering a yawn, the well-padded figure rose and stroked the contended tabby before padding toward the stairs. "Don't be long, and don't disturb our new arrival."

"No, ma'am." The generous woman had recently hired, Sundown, the hippified grandson of a friend, and given him the middle bedroom. Of course, Evie was stuck with the creepy one on the end.

Heaven forbid she should disrupt his beauty sleep, though it might be fun to bother him a little, give him a taste of what she endured every night. Nix that, he would discover soon enough.

Huddled on the couch with the cat, she closed her

eyes, trying to block the indiscernible voices speaking in hushed fragments. This old house had far more history than she'd realized. Maybe something from the past was left undone, or *someone* with unfinished business lingered... She'd bet her grandmother knew far more than she had let on.

Chimes again. The clock sounding twelve roused Evie.

Dang it. She'd dozed off on the couch. She had better brave the stairs before Grandma G. reappeared. Gladys McIntyre was a force of nature.

Rain fell, and a cool breeze blew through cracked windows. Evie took the lacy pink crocheted coverlet from the back of the couch and draped it around her shoulders, blinking with fatigue. Loose brown hair spilled down her back, the spray of lavender still pinned to the braid looped on her head. She had masses of hair to play with. Dressing up Victorian style was Grandma G.'s idea to draw visitors. She called Evie 'the belle of Lavender and Lace Herb Farm.'

Visitors wanted their pictures taken with her, especially in the carriage. Her business-minded grandmother also kept several gorgeous horses and offered carriage rides. The praise guests heaped on Evie was flattering, really, if her heart would stop pounding.

"Goodnight, Tiddles." No way would that cat come with her. She'd tried to bring him before, *once,* and gotten a nasty scratch. What did it mean when she was going where cats feared to tread?

Hiking up her skirts, she trailed across the room, and ascended the shadowy staircase. The pattering on the tin roof partly masked her footfall, but no matter how carefully she placed her laced shoes, the steps emitted telling creaks. She halted partway down the hall, swallowing past the lump of fear in her throat, when the voices grew louder. Realizing where she was, she sighed. What if Sundown discovered her creeping past his door like a frightened pup?

'Sunny Boy,' as she'd dubbed the ponytailed blond, had gone to bed early after a long day harvesting lavender blossoms. One of many days here, he probably thought.

Wrong. He wouldn't last. Live-in help never did. Sooner or later, the house spooked them. The final glimpse she'd had of the guy before him was a car peeling out of the driveway. He'd even left some of his clothes behind. Most of the staff commuted.

There. At the end of the hall, illuminated by a mini nightlight she had plugged into an outlet, was her bedroom. She managed to walk to the door before stopping again.

None of her friends believed her about *the whispers*, or the presence she sensed. She had no doubt ghosts were real after passing her late grandfather on the steps one evening, but friends insisted everything was in her head, citing her legendary imagination. Easy to do when they hadn't spent the night here. Somehow, it never suited anyone to stay over. *Chickens.*

Just wait until the whispers call you, Sunny Boy.

She took a steadying breath, turned the brass knob, and stepped into the room. The fragrance of lavender greeted her. Grandma G. had tucked sachets under her mattress to help her sleep and left small cloth bags in the drawers of an antique dresser. A sachet of apricot scented agrimony lay beneath her pillow.

This age-old herb was thought to induce slumber

and offer protection against the dark forces. Other powerful herbs scented the room. Angelica, St. John's Wort, and sage were in the bunch on the bedside stand beside the antique brass lamp with an ornamental white shade.

The walk-in, but duck your head, closet at the far side of the room summoned her. Boxes of Christmas decorations, a Santa, and reindeer figures stored inside the slanted nook partially hid the steps leading to the attic and the presence she swore was there. She hadn't encountered the being in question. Yet. It wasn't cool for a nineteen-year-old to harbor terrors of a closet, but she did.

She threw her hands up after a particularly loud summons. "What do you want from me?"

There was a rap on the downstairs door.

Chapter Two

Startled by the knock on the front door, Evie hurriedly retraced her steps, nearly stumbling in the blackness. The nightlight in the hall must have gone out. She clung to the railing to descend the stairs.

Why were moonbeams the only illumination in the parlor? She'd left the lamp on. Tiddles couldn't turn it off.

Guided by the milky light coming through the windows, she made her way to the door. When had it stopped raining?

More importantly, should she open at a stranger's knock? What if he—she sensed their caller was male—had *foul play*, as police dramas termed it, on his mind? She didn't even have pepper spray. Where was her grandmother?

"Open up. I need to get to cover," urged a masculine voice in a gruff whisper.

What? Who? She turned the lock and cracked the door.

He peered through the slit she'd made. "Is that you, Hettie?"

Was he seeking one of the girls on staff? The name wasn't familiar, but it might be the part-timer Grandma G. recently took on. Hesitant, but intrigued, Evie widened the opening.

A tall young man stood before her in a brown

wide-brimmed hat and jacket that fell below his waist. Shoulder length hair ruffled in the breeze. Dark pants met chestnut-colored riding boots, and he wore buff leather gloves. Moonlight streamed over the lean figure.

Angel light.

He didn't smell angelic, but of wood smoke and days in the saddle, part horse, part man, and the wide-open outdoors. His pungent masculine blend was unknown to her, but she recognized the elements...wind, fire, horse, and man.

Did cowboys live around here?

From what she could see of his face, he wasn't bad looking, and he returned her stare. Clearly, he had anticipated someone else answering his knock.

The stranger shook his head as if to wake himself, a rueful smile on his face. "Are you gonna keep me on the porch until Sam Hobbs finds me? The last guide he caught was shot before he said his prayers."

Alarm rifled through her. "No. Sorry." Baffled almost beyond coherent speech, she stepped aside to allow him passage.

He shut the door behind them and locked it. A swift pivot and he had her upper arm in his grip. She gasped as he pulled her back.

His gloved hand pressed her skin where the coverlet had slipped down past her short, ruffled sleeves, distracting her. "Don't stand near the door or a window. Hobbs might shoot you, too."

Air escaped her in shallow pants. "Dear God, why?"

"Shhh." The cowboy went still, his body taut beside hers.

She was rigid with dread, her heart thudding

against her ribs. Did she hear a twig snap? *No.* It must be her imagination.

The night was eerily quiet. Somewhere a dog barked. An owl hooted.

Seconds stretched into minutes, until she finally whispered. "Is he gone?"

"Not sure." Her companion crept to the window.

He remained motionless at the glass, watching, waiting. "Don't see anything," he said at last, pulling off his gloves.

She exhaled heavily. "Shouldn't you carry a gun, if this man's after you?"

He turned, leaving his gloves on the windowsill. "What?"

"My father says you have the right to protect yourself." Wasn't that the cowboy creed?

She grew aware of him scrutinizing her again.

"You are suggesting I shoot Hobbs?" Incredulity underlay his tone.

She wasn't advocating murder. "No, but before Hobbs shoots you, or is caught, maybe carrying a gun is a good idea, that's all I'm saying." An odd conversation to have with someone this overtly masculine. "Or maybe we should call the sheriff?"

"No need, miss." He patted his left side beneath the jacket. "I have a revolver. But Mennonites object to my shooting men on their land. You're not one of the plain people, are you?"

Her jaw dropped, an ache building behind her eyes. "Not remotely. Why on earth would you think I was?"

"This is a Mennonite house."

"*Was*," she emphasized, confused. Who was this guy?

He jerked as if stung. "Were they run off the farm?" he asked, his voice sharp.

"No. The property changed hands legally. But it was years ago." What was this dude going on about?

"Not possible. I was here only last week, and everything was normal. As much as it can be, considering." He sounded in dead earnest.

Had she missed the apocalypse memo? Was this an insane joke? The ache in her head grew, a strange buzz in her ears.

"Who are you?" He walked toward her, the floor creaking under his boots.

She panicked and scrambled back, almost falling over a stool. Who rearranged the room, and when?

Scant time to wonder with him advancing on her.

"Evie McIntyre." Her voice hitched an octave higher. "Who are you? Who's Hobbs? Did my grandmother hire you to patrol the place? Are we in danger? It's always been so peaceful here."

"Until it's not."

Crap. She should have taken that martial arts class her dad had mentioned several weeks ago.

The cowboy closed the space between them, his presence unlike any other man she knew. Greater, somehow. He emitted far more impact. Usually, she scarcely noticed guys. Now, breathing was difficult. She shook, and not only from fear.

He slid an arm around her waist to keep her upright as she tilted. His maleness charged through her like the rushing tide of a storm-tossed sea. Questions circled in the meld of sensations from *what's going on*, and *who is he*, to *holy wow*.

"Don't be alarmed, miss. I'll not harm you. No one

hired me to safeguard the farm. I'm a volunteer."

His warm breath tickled her ear and tremors ran through her. She wanted to bolt and remain close to him at the same time. "What if Hobbs had come to the house?" She berated herself, wondering why that was the only thing she could think to ask.

"I would have gone around back and led him away. Shooting him is a last resort, and then I would have his body to hide..."

A strangled "Oh," was all she managed between pants.

"Deep breaths, miss. Slow and steady. That's the way."

She attempted to do as he encouraged and failed. "I'm getting a little dizzy." Was this when you were supposed to breathe into a paper bag or something?

"Here." He firmed his grip on her and took a flask from an inside pocket. A finger of moonlight shone on the metal as he held it to her lips. "Take a good sip."

She did as he said, questioning her judgment, and choking on what must be whiskey.

He administered a second swallow. "Feeling better?"

Not a lot. She nodded, though, before he gave her any more of the fiery stuff.

He knocked back a swallow and returned the flask to his pocket. "No need for panic. Certainly, danger lurks, especially for me. It's war." His tone was grim. "Hobbs is a Rebel Scout, and a crack shot. I'm Jack Ramsey, also a crack shot, but weary of killing men." He offered a small smile when she looked at him. "To atone for my past, I became a guide, or agent."

Killing echoed in a merry-go-round of strange

words and imagery, but that wasn't her first question
"For what?"

"The Unionist Underground Railroad."

She stared at him blankly. "Say again?"

"How can you not know? You are in one of the
depots."

"Depot? This house?" she croaked, words sticking
in her throat. "You make it sound like a train station."

"In a way. The Wenger family have housed a lot of
men wanting out of this war. I help the poor wretches
escape through the mountains to the north and
freedom."

"What? Are they black? How bad have things
gotten in the country?"

"Plenty bad. Some Negroes escape with them.
Most men are pacifists who refuse to fight in any war
and are being forced into this one. Some are deserters.
Others are fleeing conscription."

"They brought the draft back?" This was it. She
had officially lost her mind.

"It never went away. Where have you been, miss?
More to the point, who are you?" His gruff demand
stirred the hair at her cheek.

She tilted her face at him. Only the barest outline
of his strong features was visible, and yet... Man, was
he hot. *Focus Evie.* "I told you. I'm Evie McIntyre. I
live here with my grandmother. Didn't you realize?"

"That so? I don't suppose you would be a spy in a
Mennonite house. Still. Never know. I best get a good
look at you."

"Who would I be spying for?"

"Rebs. Neither side wishes me well. I'm in no
man's land."

Her heart drummed wildly. "Where does that leave me?"

"That's the question, isn't it?" He steadied Evie on her feet.

Was it? She had no idea what was going on and watched dazedly as he took something from the leather pouch hanging over his shoulder. "What's that?"

"Lucifers."

He'd lost her again. There must be a powerful resistance movement at work. She didn't follow politics. Maybe she should. Had matters come to an explosive head tonight? Why hadn't her grandmother said something?

He drew what resembled matches from a small metal container and struck one. Sulphurous sparks added pungency to the room. He lit the stubby candle in a tin lantern on an end table. Shadows danced from the pale taper glowing through the punches in the metal.

Pretty, how the light made patterns on the ceiling. *Wait*. Where had that lantern come from?

The stained-glass lamp Grandma G. treasured was just there before she went to bed. *Dear God in heaven.* What had happened to the room?

Nothing in the parlor was as it had been a short while ago. Furnishings suited to a monastery had displaced the frou-frou décor. Simple wooden chairs, stools, and a plain couch were arranged in a circle. A small table supported a large black book, possibly the Bible. Discarded knitting lay on a side table. A spinning wheel sat in one corner.

There were no frills anywhere. No lavender sprigged wallpaper or lacy valentines, or anything she remembered. Her grandmother's cherished things were gone. Everything had changed, and yet, the layout of the room was the same.

Was she lost in a dream, or had she stepped into a parallel universe? That sometimes happened…in *Doctor Who,* not her world.

Oh, my," she gulped, and blindly reached out to steady herself against the back of a chair. "Not what I was expecting."

"Nor are you." The man called Jack returned the match tin to his pouch and studied her by the flickering light, his sandy brows arching under the broad brim. "Whew." He thumbed his hat back. "You're nothing like Hettie Wenger."

"Not in this life," she said in a bare whisper, realization nagging at her.

"Did you have another?"

She nodded, gazing into the most glorious greenish-brown eyes, like sun-dappled trees. W*ham.* Lightning bolt impact. She had to remember to shut her mouth, but could not stop staring at him, and he swept his admiring gaze over her.

"I haven't seen a woman as fashionably dressed as you in ages, or one as pretty. Ever. Did I die? Go to heaven?"

Her cheeks heated at the bold compliment. "With this décor?" She waved at their surroundings. "No."

Humor hinted in his face beneath the wide brim, and he rubbed a chin roughened with the beginnings of a beard. "I'm trying to place you, Miss McIntyre. Are you Wesleyan?"

Did it matter? Was he hung up on religion?

She battled to find her way through the muddled maze of her thoughts. "Do you mean Methodist?"

He inclined his head.

"No. I'm Presbyterian. The last time I was anything."

A slow smile curved his lips and crinkled his eyes. "I admire your honesty."

"Thanks. I'm usually honest." She shifted her searching gaze from his Hotness, as she already thought of him, to the room and back again. "Crazy, maybe, but truthful."

"You are not mad."

She gave him a look of disbelief.

"I'm not sure what is happening here, but not that," he said, removing his hat. He set it on a table, running his hand through hair that would be blonde with a shampoo.

He must have been in the saddle for days, and camping out, whenever he felt safe. "Nice hat. Where's your horse?" she asked randomly, trying to find some grounding in all the crazy.

He eyed her quizzically. "Tethered in the woods behind the house."

"Why there? We have a barn." At least, they did.

"Barns aren't safe with rebels on the prowl and rogue bands taking what they like. Horses are a favorite. The Wengers leave hay in the woods for me to feed Buck when I come."

"Thoughtful of them." Her voice was a tremulous murmur. Had he said *rogue bands*?

"Yes. Buck's seen me through a lot of battles and trips to the mountains. The Wengers hide their mare, foal, and draft horse there, too. They have had other horses taken, and some hogs, sheep…"

She gaped at him. "Grandma G. would be out

holding off marauders with a shotgun, and have the staff toting them, too."

His mouth narrowed in a slight frown. "Staff? You mean servants?"

"I suppose you could call them that," she said, though no one ever did.

"Not slaves?" he emphasized.

"Good Lord, no. They sometimes complain about the work, but no one's keeping them prisoner. And say what you like about Grandma's temper, she pays them well."

His shoulders sagged in apparent relief. "I don't hold with keeping slaves."

"Neither do I." What had she missed?

"My father has a few," he divulged, his eyes haunted. "But Papa's sympathies are with the Union."

Goosebumps flushed to her toes and she swallowed hard. They weren't in another dimension, or in two thousand eighteen anywhere. This was freaked out lunacy. Planets spinning out of sync. Unless she'd fallen for an elaborate hoax—unlikely—she'd traveled back to the Civil War era at Lavender and Lace Herb Farm before it was called by that name. She must have arrived in the days of its Mennonite builders.

How in the world?

There was one totally improbable, the odds astronomically against it, possibility. She'd asked the house, as had Grandma G., and the house had answered.

Better go along with it for now. Her thoughts wheeling, she faltered. "Unionist men have slaves?"

He eyed her as if she were crazy, after all. "You do realize four slave states remained in the Union?

Maryland, Delaware, Kentucky, Missouri? You've heard of these?"

"No. Yes. I mean, I didn't realize," she fumbled.

"The war has many faces, and some of them wear masks."

"Yeah. I should have paid more attention to my father, he's very interested in the War Between the States, or listened better in school."

A glint of impatience crossed the cowboy's gaze. "What does school have to do with anything? This isn't a history lesson. It's happening now."

"Right. Sorry." She racked her brain to think of what she knew of this era as her grip on the present—past?—slipped.

Questions crowded through her shock. "Your father doesn't support the Confederacy? I thought all Southerners did."

His lips tightened. "Not all. No."

"I think my ancestors did."

"Your *what*?" He regarded her as one might a mental patient.

She blanched, realizing her mistake. "Never mind. Does your father live in the valley? Is he nearby? Do you ever see him?"

Jack swiped his fingers through his hair and held up a hand like a traffic cop. "Slow down, miss. Yes. He has a large holding in the northern end of the valley. No. I haven't seen him in years. He disowned me when I enlisted."

"To fight for the Confederacy?"

"Yes. To defend my beloved homeland, Virginia."

She battled to steady her voice. "Doesn't Virginia still need you?"

He dropped his gaze to the lamp, as if its light would guide him. "Maybe so. I had my fill of war at Gettysburg, in Pickett's Charge."

The infamous name tolled a somber bell. Even *she* had heard of Gettysburg. She gripped his coat sleeve, his muscular arm firm beneath it. "Dear God. You were there? Dad said Pickett's Charge was terrible. It's amazing you survived."

He squeezed his eyes shut and froze, a tremor running through him. Then he clasped her fingers with his hand. The veneer gone, he looked at her, raw anguish in eyes shadowed by ghosts. "You're right. I shouldn't be here."

Pity swelled in her and spilled over. She squeezed his hand. "I didn't mean it that way. Yes. You should be here. Some men survived. Why not you?"

He blinked hard, dashing at the sheen in his eyes with rough knuckles. "You don't understand. Thousands of good men were killed that day. I saw them go down on every side. Heard their cries. The fallen littered the crimson ground like leaves. Some died later in agony. Our division was decimated. I can't begin to say what it was."

For a long moment, neither of them spoke. His face said it all. "No. I suppose not," she whispered.

"Why did I live, and they did not?"

"Only God can answer that. How did you make it out alive?"

He tapped his right leg. "I was hit in the charge partway across the field. Two men helped me off, and they were struck, too. We staggered together, dragging ourselves. Others came to our aid. I was fortunate not to lose my leg and pondered my survival on the hellish retreat to Virginia and during my recovery in the hospital in Harrisonburg."

"What then?" she asked softly.

"Being an officer, I tried to carry on as expected, but fell ill. I was given leave and sent home to recover. Only, I didn't have a home to return to."

"Where did you go?"

"I'm not sure where I was heading, but the Wengers found me fallen by my horse near their farm, out of my head with fever. They brought me here and nursed me back to health. I confessed my doubts regarding the cause and they told me of the Unionist Underground Railroad. I don't need to escape Virginia. I can survive in the mountains, hunting and bartering. I built a cabin there and help men caught in this unholy war to get out."

Wonder washed over her. "Unbelievable. How many have you helped?"

"One hundred and twenty," he said matter-of-factly.

She had to remember not to gape at him. "Don't you see? They might have died without you. Is your father proud now?"

He gave a hoarse laugh. "I am dead to him."

"But you've come back to his way of thinking?"

"No. I'm not siding with the Union, just against this ongoing blood bath, and my father's not the forgiving sort." Bitterness edged his tone.

"Have you tried going to him?"

Pain glazed his eyes. "No point. I know how it is with him."

"I'm truly sorry."

"Thanks." Emotion roughened his voice and he

shifted from boot to boot, as if uncomfortable at the unmanly display.

Evie became aware they were still holding hands and slid her fingers from his. "You must miss your family," she offered, unsure of what else to say.

"Yes. And friends battling on, if they are still alive. I lost most of them at Gettysburg. But there are men here to aid. Some are mere boys."

For such a young man, he was old in experience. Years beyond her. "How old are you, Jack?"

He arched his brows at her familiar use of his name. "Twenty-two, Miss McIntyre."

"Please, call me Evie. After this much sharing, I think first names are appropriate."

Shrugging broad shoulders, he nodded. "Fine by me. No need to stand on formality. I don't expect I shall survive this war."

Pain twinged in her at the thought of him dying. "I pray that's not so. Shouldn't the war be winding down?" She couldn't remember exactly how long it lasted.

"Lord only knows, dear lady. I confess to feeling a bit more hopeful in your sweet presence. And what of you, Evie?" He smoothed her cheek with callused fingertips and inhaled. "You even smell like a thousand flowers."

"Roses, jasmine, iris…" she whispered.

"You are an angel come to this bloody earth."

"There's a reason for that."

He groaned. "Don't tell me you are a spirit? You feel real."

"I'm as real as you. Only…" How could she tell him?

"What?" he pressed.

She took a deep breath and exhaled. "I'm from the future."

His eyes widened.

A sense of urgency welled in her and she bent toward him. "Please believe me. It's the only explanation. I live in this house. I swear I do. But tonight, everything has changed. And you're here talking about the Civil War like it's now. But it was over one hundred and fifty years ago for me."

Words tumbled from her as she sought to alter his silent stare. "Seriously, Jack. There's always been something odd about this place, like the house is trying to tell me something. And my grandmother told me it used to belong to a Mennonite family named Wenger and—"

Creaking steps intruded on their hushed conversation.

"Shhh." He held a finger to her lips before she had a clue if he believed a thing she'd said, or thought she was completely insane.

They both glanced around. An older man with a gray beard and long white nightshirt descended the stairs. He halted on the bottom step in his stocking feet and surveyed them from beneath a grizzled brow that matched his rumpled hair.

He brushed back his untidy locks with a work-worn hand, and goggled at her, then turned to Jack. "I did not think to see you this night, Jack Ramsey. Who have you there? Never, have I laid eyes on such a grand refugee woman. Who is this *Englischer*?"

His jaw tight, Jack swiveled from the astonished man to Evie. Everything in him seemed to be weighing her.

He'd called her an angel. He must see her sincerity? She pleaded with her eyes for him to take her side.

He seemed to come to a decision and clasped her hand in his. "This lady isn't a refugee. She is with me."

Relief roiled through her churning gut.

"*Ach.*" A smile deepened the creases on the older man's face, like the wrinkles in a shrunken apple. "Have you taken a wife, as my Mary advised?"

"I have, Paul. The minister was in western Virginia. I thought to surprise you with my lovely new bride."

A blow to her middle could scarcely have left Evie more winded. Opening and closing her mouth, she gaped at Jack.

"You surely did." The newcomer clucked and shook a thickened finger at him. "You are a cagey one, Jack. Keeping this lady a secret, and wedding at such a time as this."

"The perfect time. Let me introduce you to Evie Ramsey."

"*Hallo. Wie bischt du,*" the man called Paul hailed her, likely a Pennsylvania Dutch greeting.

She nodded weakly and almost sank to the floor. Jack's arm around her waist was all that kept her standing.

"It's the only way," he whispered in her ear. "Or you will be sent to God alone knows where, if word gets out. Maybe prison for being a spy. Or an asylum."

"I'm not a spy or crazy. Do you believe what I said?" she hissed.

"Still thinking."

"What?" she sputtered. "I told you the truth." Lightheadedness rushed over her. "My head's whirling."

"I'll see to you," he assured her, circling an arm around her waist. "What say we celebrate, Paul?" he called more loudly. "My bride could use a hot drink."

Their apparent host nodded his readiness. "I regret we have no *kaffi* to serve. Roasted chicory we have aplenty. Needs must."

"We all sorely miss coffee but are warmed by your hospitality. And Paul, just so you know how special this occasion is. It's our wedding night," Jack added, firming his grip on Evie.

She slumped against Jack at Paul's answering chuckle. *This can't be happening.*

Chapter Three

Masking his incredulity, Jack Ramsey considered the stunned young woman he upheld with an arm snugged around her middle. If he removed his support, she'd slump to the floor, and that was the last thing he wanted. Discovering Evie McIntyre in the Wenger farmhouse was as far-fetched as finding a pot of gold in the woodpile. He wasn't letting her go.

Damn, she was mesmerizing.

God help him. She rocked his world to its molten core.

The sight and feel of her kindled a fire in him. Her perfume fanned the flames, imbuing his senses like the headiest love potion. He wouldn't accuse her of witchcraft, but she was an enchantress, whether she realized it or not. The bemusement in her blue-gray eyes told him she didn't have an inkling of the earthshaking impact she wrought on him. He'd never reached the heights she unwittingly beckoned him to, and he had no business attempting the ascension now.

Hell. There was a war on. Possibly forever.

Strange how unaware she was of the strife pitting brother against brother and tearing families apart. Where had she been? Surely, not the future, as she claimed.

Unless someone dwelled in a cave, they could not possibly be this unaffected, and she was no cave

27

dweller. Her hands were soft against his, her cheeks like petals, and her gown the finest he'd seen since prewar life with a prosperous father.

As delightful as diversion with her would be, he had committed himself to aiding the unfortunates caught in this brutal struggle. His work was not yet done, and he must tread with care. Nearly every man's bullet had his name on it, as happens when you abandon one cause and don't embrace the other.

There was another problem with the tempting dalliance, apart from the fact that he and Evie were not truly united in holy wedlock. He wasn't sure she was right in the head. In fact, he was increasingly certain she wasn't, even though he had said otherwise.

"Did you suffer a blow?" he whispered in her ear. Maybe the effects would pass, and she'd come to her senses.

A hint of annoyance penetrated the fog that seemed to envelope her. "Before or after you announced our wedding night?" she thrust back, while their enlivened host hastened up the creaking stairs to alert the family to their arrival.

The floorboards overhead sounded beneath Paul's tread, and he rapped on doors. "Guests! Our friend, Jack Ramsey, has brought his new wife. Wake, my dear Mary. Make haste, my girls. Hurry and dress Hettie, Margaret, Lena, Sara! Come and greet them, Anna, Faith, and Joy."

The amazement in Evie's eyes heightened and she glanced at Jack as if she couldn't believe her ears. "How many daughters does he have?"

"Seven. Two sets of twins."

"Good Lord," she exclaimed under her breath. "It's

like *Seven Brides for Seven Brothers*."

"What?"

"The old-fashioned musical. Well, it's old to me. You might better know the term *musical theater*? Anyway, *Seven Brides for Seven Brothers* is being revived. Never mind—"

"It's quite all right," he interjected, before she grew even more breathless. "Your musical sounds most diverting. So many fortunate brothers. The Wenger sisters love to sing and will descend on us with a chorus of questions."

She narrowed her eyes at him. "Which you had better have answers for, Mister *liar liar pants on fire*."

He smiled wryly at the childish rhyme. "I am an adept dissembler. Follow my lead."

"I think I'd better sit down."

"Of course. Allow me." He assisted her to the couch and helped her settle on the rust-colored upholstery.

She ran her fingers over the fabric. "*Horsehair*?"

Odd question, but she was unusual, to say the least. "Most folk have horsehair if they have anything. Easy to come by and durable."

She squinted at him thoughtfully. "My grandmother's couch is velvet, but I recall the term from an antique show she likes."

Maybe he should just nod in response to these fantasies.

Sighing, she leaned her forehead on her hand. "I know what you're thinking about me, Jack."

"Doubtful." Thoughts tumbled through him in a fiery meld of *I want to take you in my arms, fair lady, and kiss you,* to *What on God's green earth are you talking about, woman?*

"I am not concussed," she continued, addressing her lap while seemingly awaiting his reply.

"Nothing that severe," he assured her, with strong suspicions to the contrary.

Wondering how near he dared sit to this exquisite, baffling female, he lowered himself at her side, as they were supposedly newlywed. Heat shot through him at their close proximity. What a thrill just to be near her. He burned to be nearer still.

Reining himself in, he battled to recall the topic under discussion. "I'm merely saying a blow might account for your confusion."

She glanced narrowly at him through her fingers. "You mean, I was knocked silly and dreamed up a life in this house with my grandma, every facet of which I could describe to you?"

He'd wager she possessed imagination enough. "I've heard some mighty peculiar ramblings from injured men."

"With head wounds, you mean?" Her frown deepened. "I suppose you think I also dreamed up my mom and dad, plus a younger sister, and two little brothers?"

"They might be real. Just not in the future," he suggested, contemplating a clan of McIntyre's.

"How do you account for no sign of injury on me? Look for yourself."

His lips twitched at her invitation. "Through that wealth of hair?"

She waved him on.

"You don't have to invite me twice." He slid his fingers through the honey-streaked brown lengths rippling around her in a glorious mane. She'd even tucked lavender blossoms in the narrow braid circled on her head. Intoxicating. Ribbons of heat zinged through him.

Steady, he cautioned himself, and lightly pressed her scalp. No lumps or bumps. She didn't wince from a recent bruise. If she were hurt, she gave no indication.

"Perfection," he breathed out. And the opposite of what he'd witnessed in camp and on the battlefield. "You are as fresh as a spring morn sparkling with dew."

Her cheeks pinkened. "Easily done with hot and cold running water at the turn of a faucet."

A strange way to evade a compliment. "Of what do you speak?"

"Bathrooms with showers. Toilets that flush. No outhouse or chamber pots."

He drew back at this latest revelation. "Are you among the wealthiest of the land?"

"No. These amenities are common where I'm from."

"Nae," he argued. "I have heard of pipes carrying water and toilets that flush, but only those with the greatest means have bathrooms and water closets. The rest make do with privies and chamber pots, or the screen of a tree or bush."

"I could show you modern things, if you return with me."

He arched his brows at her. "Journey to another realm? How is that possible?"

She pursed rose-blushed lips. "I don't know."

Nor did he, but he hung on her every move. Perhaps she was vastly wealthy. She must be, with her expensive clothes and talk of theater and running water.

But if that were so, why was she in the Wenger farm house in the middle of a war?

"I confess I marvel at you and detect no injury." He snatched at possibilities. "Perhaps illness confuses you?"

"Am I feverish? Are my eyes glassy?"

He laid his hand on her creamy brow and couldn't resist cupping her cheek. "Not in the least. Only as bewildered as I feel."

She searched his eyes. "Can you say how I came to be here?"

"No." He reluctantly withdrew his hand. "That is the great puzzle."

"To us both. So, don't go thinking I'm good with it." She fought to still the quaver in her voice, the struggle evident in her face. "The house did this."

"What do you mean, *the house*?"

"I told you it's a strange place, with secretive voices I call *the whispers*. They are the most vocal in the closet."

He studied her closely. "Where?"

"In my bedroom upstairs at the end of the hall. There are two rooms on the left, plus a bathroom, and then there's me on the end."

"Yes." He envisioned the second story layout. She had it correct minus the bathroom. "There's no closet in that chamber. The attic door opens from the far side."

"It still does, only through the closet now…" She trailed off, then firmed her quivering chin and met his close regard. A look of clarity had displaced the mystification in her eyes. "I haven't heard *the whispers* since going back in time. That must be significant. Whatever message they're trying to send me involves an event that has not yet occurred."

"And what might that be?"

"Not sure, but I'm onto something important, Jack."

He gave a nod as if appreciative of her discovery Better that way. It would keep her calmer, he hoped.

Before she related further fantastical theories, the quick footfall on the stairs announced they were about to be interrupted. Everything she'd asserted was outlandish, save one. Her presence here. He couldn't account for it, yet there must be a rational explanation.

She had the soft Virginia accent of the Shenandoah Valley, southern in tone but not overly prominent. Maybe she'd been transported to the house by carriage and left on the porch for her own safety, and unknowingly found her way inside?

Talk about bizarre. Why would anyone do that?

How important was she? Judging by her elegant appearance, very. But to whom?

Perhaps, he was meant to protect her...

She should have come bearing a letter of instruction pinned to her lacy pink wrap.

Scant time to ponder the mystery that was Evie McIntyre. A flurry of brown and blue skirts swirled into the room amid scents of homemade soap and herbal water.

What a contrast she made to the Wenger sisters. Ranging in age from twelve to twenty, the girls were plainly dressed as befit their simple lives. Rosy faces, dotted with freckles and creased in smiles, beamed at the couple. They wore their ginger and coppery colored hair in plaited braids or on their heads under white caps. No frills. No ribbons. None of the finery adorning Evie.

He wouldn't describe them as beauties, but they were pleasing to look on and always lifted his spirits. Hettie's bright blue eyes were particularly agreeable. Their petite mother was gowned in black and stood by their string bean father.

After being caught in his nightshirt, Paul had donned a black 'sack' suit with trousers, vest, and a coat that hung on his slim frame. A smile curved Mary's weathered countenance, gray tendrils escaping her black cap. Though goodhearted, she possessed an outspoken nature for a plain woman and could be what Jack termed belligerently affectionate.

He sprang to his feet in deference to the families' arrival while anticipating free flowing speech from the matron of the house. Offering a short bow, he smiled at the assembly.

"Ladies, I apologize for disturbing your slumber. How kind of you to make us welcome." He gestured at the young woman seated in doe-like shock. "Allow me to introduce my bride, Evie Ramsey."

As soon as the words left his lips, the crazy thought passed through his mind that he wished they were true. Madness. He'd be rambling like a lunatic next thing. He lowered his gaze and saw she needed a nudge to play her part in this facade.

He reached toward her. "Say hello, sweetheart."

She clasped his fingers and he helped her to rise. Seeming more in command of herself, she extended her free hand. "How do you do? I'm pleased to meet you."

The girls pressed her fingers, murmuring well wishes, and darting awed glances at the exotic newcomer. Jack recognized *Gott segen eich,* God bless you, in the blend of English and Low German. He'd picked up some of their words and expressions, but his ancestry was Scots-Irish, totally different. It made the friendship between them that much more remarkable.

Mary surveyed the bridal pair with satisfaction in her brown eyes. "Did I not say you should take a wife, and here she stands? Good work, Jack Ramsey. *Gut Gut*." She nodded happily. "Welcome to you and your new bride. God keep you both and bless you with joy, long life, and plentiful children."

Evie inhaled at the well-intentioned wish and coughed. Jack noted her change the choking to throat clearing. Fortunately, she didn't launch into a coughing fit. Having abundant fertility wished on the unsuspecting girl might send her into one.

He smothered a smile, but Mary wasn't finished.

"For children are a blessing from God in this troubled world," she continued, a quizzical eye on the young bride, as if she feared her not mindful of her blessings and duties.

"*Ya*," her husband agreed, while their daughters tittered good-naturedly. "Am I not eternally grateful for my girls, and the sons you helped shift from harm, Jack Ramsey?"

He sidled self-consciously. "The least I could do."

Paul shook off his effort. "You got my boys to safety in the north, and there they shall stay until this terrible war is through. I shall never forget the good service you did us."

For simple people, they were heaping it on. Jack felt his cheeks warm under the homage.

"Nor I," Mary assured him. "We will always remember your kindness and courage." Her daughters also appeared duly obliged to him for their brothers' safety.

The three boys were sorely missed, especially at planting and harvest time, but the girls were hard workers. Mennonites raised their children to love God and work.

"May God keep Stephen, John, and Luke safe and bring them home soon," Jack offered, as blessings were flying around him.

"*Amen.*" Paul blinked at the sheen in his blue eyes. "We are giving you and your wife the chamber at the far end of the hall for as long as you have need. The girls will fetch towels, fresh water, food, and that hot drink you requested for a late wedding supper. If we had received word of your marriage sooner, we would have roasted a turkey." He brightened. "Tomorrow."

No barrage of questions? Jack was pleasantly surprised. "Thank you."

Mary made a shooing gesture. "Off with you. We'll not keep you standing about entertaining us on your wedding night."

Evie startled beside him. "But your own sleep—"

The refusal in their hostess's eyes and squared jaw cut her short. "Will keep until we've properly seen to you two."

What choice had Jack other than to comply, with the family looking on, expectation writ in their honest faces? He couldn't insist he'd sleep on the floor and send Evie upstairs alone. Besides, he didn't object to accompanying her, even though he should by all that was decent. He wouldn't harm her, and must keep an eye on his charge, which she had apparently become. He had no idea what else to do with her.

This night was turning out vastly differently than

the encounter he'd anticipated with Sam Hobbs. The irksome hound was probably waiting for him out in the fields, or camped beneath a canopy of trees, or behind a rocky outcropping in the not-too-distant mountains. Meanwhile, Jack was sharing a bed with the most beautiful woman he'd ever seen.

How Sam would howl if he knew. He stifled a chuckle at the irony fate had handed him.

Sobering under the avid gaze of the onlookers, he took Evie's arm. "Come, wife," he said, with a respectful nod at the assembly. "Let us leave these kind people and retire to the chamber they have graciously allowed us."

He didn't dare risk a glance at her. They were headed for the very room he'd heard so much about, and not remotely in the manner he expected she would wish to visit it with him. If she cared to go there with him at all.

She gathered her full skirts and he escorted her across the parlor. The quiver he detected told him she didn't want to venture there in any manner whatsoever. Did the *whispers* she'd spoken of alarm her? She'd said they were gone now. Did she fear their return? Difficult to discern what was going on in her head at any given moment.

"Guten nacht!" chorused after them as they climbed the steps.

"Good night!" he called over his shoulder.

"See you in a bit with food and warm water," Mary reminded him, lest he forget they would soon traipse after him and Evie.

He signaled his understanding. *"Denki!"* he rejoined, using the German for thank you. That should gratify their hostess.

Evie was mute. Likely, the Wengers thought her shy. Maybe she was, but she hadn't struck Jack that way. She'd had plenty to say to him earlier. No doubt, he would hear more shortly.

A candle flickered on the stand at the top of the stairs, casting shadows on the white walls and illuminating her pale face. "We're still in the past," she said in a small voice.

"My present," he indulged her.

"I thought time might change when we mounted the stairs."

He'd never expected that. "Take you back to the future?"

She tilted her head at him, her eyes crinkled. "I get what that means now."

"You are way ahead of me." He was pondering how to convince the celebratory family they were consummating their union, as expected, while remaining apart in the same bed...

First, their wedding supper.

An ache in his gut betrayed his wish that it truly was their special night. Apart from friends like the Wengers, and the brief companionship of the men he guided through the mountains, his life was solitary. Wives did not simply appear. Whatever Evie might be, she was totally unique, and he tightened his hold on her.

The chamber she dreaded lay straight ahead, its shadowy door revealed by candlelight. He gestured at it. "Shall we?"

She straightened her shoulders. "Brace yourself."

"Think I can brave it. I was in Pickett's Charge." Nothing could ever touch that.

Chapter Four

Like a butterfly soaring between the future and the past, Evie had swiftly arrived in the nineteenth century with no clue how long she was staying. A while longer, it would seem. Maybe indefinitely. And now, here she was poised before her former bedroom door with her pretend husband, Jack Ramsey.

She never saw that coming, or him. He'd swept her up in a whirlwind of heart-pounding thrills and the deepest shock imaginable.

Had Grandma G. missed her yet, or was she sound asleep? A pang of guilt jarred her. The goodhearted woman would be worried sick to discover her granddaughter absent from the house which, weirdly, she'd remained in. No one at either end of this bizarre journey would believe she'd bridged time, but she made no protest at being escorted by the handsome cowboy, even if he'd shamelessly announced their wedding night. And that didn't trouble her conscience the way it should.

The upstairs hallway appeared as it must have done over one hundred and fifty years ago. The boards creaking beneath her feet might be the same heart pine floor she'd walked on earlier tonight, unless the wood had been replaced since these early years. Little else remained the same as the house she'd known a short while ago.

No framed family portraits or flowery prints hung on the white plaster walls Grandma G. had painted a pale mauve. None of her grandmother's teddy bear collection overflowed wicker baskets or an heirloom cradle. A similar wooden trunk as hers, minus the pile of decorative pillows the pillow-mad woman heaped on, might also contain winter blankets. This was it for similarities, apart from the herbal scents. These were timeless.

She caught the spicy minty blend of sage, horehound, and catmint. Someone must be fighting a cold and sore throat. She hoped none of the Wenger sisters had abandoned their sickbed for her, nor did she want to occupy it if they had. The girls appeared in robust health. Maybe the herbal treatment was a success, or perhaps they'd nursed one of the boys the family had concealed, and the scent lingered.

Immersed in the past, Evie gripped Jack's left arm while he extended his right hand to the bedroom doorknob. *The whispers* were silent, but she was certain their origin lay behind the paranormal presence she'd sensed in the present-day version of the house. The question was what event had transpired to create this phenomenon, when had it occurred, and who did it involve? The presence was distinctly male.

Another thought occurred. What if Jack had something to do with the fragmented voice she'd heard? Had she been sent back to intervene for him? Given the tide of emotion swelling in her at his every look, touch, and gesture it seemed as if she had come for this exact purpose.

Wait. Was he in even greater danger than he knew? The present risk was plenty. Alarm tolled in her, and she swiveled her head at him.

He glanced down at her, arching his sandy brows. "What troubles you now?"

How could she explain? "I'm not sure yet."

"Neither am I, sweetheart." He lingered over the endearment as if he meant it.

Could he actually be falling for her, or was this part of his act? The Wengers were scrambling to be good hosts, heating water and food to carry up to the newlyweds. He didn't need to pretend to be married until they reappeared.

Maybe he really was attracted to her, though she was fairly certain he considered her mental. Perhaps he didn't hold little things like insanity against a girl? Maybe on some deeper, nearly subconscious level, he believed her?

She'd had boyfriends, briefly; some older than her. None of those guys remotely resembled the man at her side. They didn't make men like Jack anymore.

Was there any way to keep him?

Maybe… The strength of her wish surprised her.

Her thoughts whirring, she stayed as she was, her gaze fixed on his. The candle on the stand outside the door wavered in a cool breeze. She instinctively clutched her shawl as he returned her scrutiny above the dancing shadows.

Curiosity mixed with the admiration hinting in his eyes. He smiled encouragingly and flung open the door. "Look. Is this chamber so very terrifying?"

The bare bones of her bedroom lay behind the simply furnished space. Against one white wall stood a well-crafted bed frame, also a double size like hers, though not a four-poster bed such as she had. While she slept beneath a brightly colored quilt purchased at a Mennonite auction, this mattress was covered in a comforter pieced from scraps of somber clothing.

Beside the bed was a stand with a glowing white candle on it; another large trunk occupied the space at its foot. A linen washstand with a brown stoneware pitcher and basin, and narrow rod for draping hand towels, banked one wall. A slim cot stretched beyond it. She questioned if Jack might sleep there, and, just as quickly, concluded she didn't want him to.

She scanned the far side of the room for the dreaded closet. A tall wooden dresser with six drawers had taken its place. She remembered him saying there was no closet in here, but the attic must remain—the creepy heart of the house.

She gestured at the wall. "Where's the attic door?"

"Behind the dresser. That weighty piece must be pushed aside to open the door. The Wengers shut it behind any men hidden up there and shove the dresser back into place."

"It's a well concealed hideout," she agreed. "But does this mean the men can't get out on their own?"

He shook his head. "The dresser is heavy and wedges the door tightly. But no one poking around in the house will discover them, as long as they keep still."

"The fire marshal would have something to say about it."

His eyes creased in a puzzled expression. "Who?"

She was using unfamiliar terms again and started to wave aside his query, then stopped, her hand still upheld. Cold realization slammed her, as if she'd been rolled in the icy surf. *Of course.* The origin of *the whispers* was painfully clear.

"Dear God," she blurted, clapping a palm to her forehead, and clutching her middle.

Jack scrutinized her, his brow furrowed, eyes searching. "What?"

Speaking was difficult in the dread sweeping through her, and she partly hunched over. "He's afraid to call out loud."

"Which *he*? Who are you speaking of?"

She pointed a trembling finger at the attic. "A man or boy is trapped up there."

"Not now he isn't."

Her heart thudded in assurance of the chill truth. "No. But he will be. Maybe more than one. I've never been sure if *the whispers* belong to a single individual."

A mix of concern and confusion clouded Jack's gaze. "You aren't making any sense."

"Not yet. I'm trying to figure this all out." A strident question occurred to her. "I could kick myself for not asking before, but what is today's date?"

"I'm not sure of the exact day." He brushed back his shoulder length hair and regarded her closely. "Mid-September, maybe later, eighteen sixty-four. Why?"

"Worse and worse." She resisted the urge to tug at his sleeve and rush him from the house. The only way back to the future lay here, if the journey was even an option for him.

He bent nearer to her. "Why does the date matter?"

Her mind wheeling, gut churning, she battled to snatch partially recalled fragments of history from her memory. Her father had told her, so had Grandma G., more than once.

"It should matter more than it does, and would, if I could just remember what happens *when*. I know late

September into October eighteen sixty-four is nightmarish in the valley. The season explains why the night air is cool, though. I thought it was June, like in the future, and I can't see outside to tell the difference. Oh, man. I've got something important to tell you but don't know where to begin—"

"Evie." He gripped her shoulders in his firm clasp. "Calm down and tell me what's going on." His voice was stern, and his demeanor sharp, the officer in him showing.

"Sheridan's coming," she gasped.

He stared at her, his mouth ajar. *"Major General Sheridan?* The Union commander?"

"Who else?"

"How do you know his name?" Jack pressed. "You were a bit hazy on the war earlier."

"Sheridan is hated in the valley to this day. My day, I mean. I'm not sure exactly when The Burning begins, but it's in late September."

"Burning?" He tightened his grip on her shoulders.

She gulped past the lump in her throat. "Sheridan's going to torch barns, outbuildings, mills, harvested corn, wheat, stacks of hay, and a lot of houses. He'll kill cows, sheep, pigs, chickens. Anything. Everything. What he doesn't burn or kill, he'll take. Horses will be rounded up. Any food he doesn't destroy goes with his men. There won't be a single chicken or cow left even for families with lots of children."

Jack paled beneath his tanned skin. "Dear Lord, Evie. You make it sound like the end of the world."

"For people living here, it will be. The cries of mothers and children will make no difference. Their pleas will fall on deaf ears."

For a long moment, he weighed her terrible revelation, revulsion tightening his mouth and eyes. "I'm not saying it cannot happen, that the Union won't bring hard war to civilians and target our green valley. Lord knows folk on both sides of this heinous conflict have suffered violence. But how do you know?"

"My dad and grandmother told me, and we learned in school. Families with deep roots here don't forget The Burning."

Lips pursed, he regarded her with a skeptical glint. "I need more to go on to be certain."

"More than the ravings of a crazy woman, you mean?" She gestured at the walls, her sweeping hand encompassing the land around them. "By the time you have more information the valley will be in flames. Sheridan burns it in thirteen fateful days. Only the parts his men overlook, or the farms a decent officer under him chooses to spare, will remain untouched."

"No." Jack shook his head at her as if he'd seen a specter.

In a way, she was one, an apparition from the future bearing warning. Only she was quite real, as was the awful event she foretold. Somehow, she must convince him.

He dropped his hands from her shoulders, raked his hair, and clenched his fists. "I do not keep abreast of every skirmish and battle," he said, pacing in a small circle. "Though I admit to admiration for those cadets who held off the invading army at New Market in May, keeping Billy Yank out of the valley."

"Yes." The reminder of their courage heartened her. "I've visited the New Market battlefield with my father. It's a museum now. And each year, the Virginia

Military Cadets read out the names of the boys killed in the battle to honor their memory." She lowered her voice. "'Put the boys in, and may God forgive me for the order.' It's what General Breckenridge said when he had to send the cadets in or lose the battle."

Jack stopped abruptly and turned toward her, astonishment in his face. "How do you know all this?"

"I told you," she said softly.

He shook his head, wonder in his eyes. "I don't know if you are from the future, but maybe you can see it."

"I can. Because it's my past."

Waving her to silence, he continued. "Say you're right, and somehow you can predict what's about to take place, what will happen to the Wengers?"

A shadow fell over her momentary elation. "They lose everything."

He tensed. "What do you mean by *everything*?"

"Their barn is burned to the ground and their crops are taken or destroyed. The same for the livestock. This house is set ablaze and badly damaged. Anyone remaining inside would quickly succumb to the smoke." Fresh alarm washed over her. "Whatever you do, don't hide in the attic."

"Why would I?"

"I have no idea, but don't send any more refugees up there. He's coming, Jack. Sheridan's coming." She sucked in a shuddering breath.

Jack gathered her to his chest, enveloping her in the primal scents of wind, fire, horse, and man, and his warm strength. "You tell an appalling bedtime tale. Why are the Mennonites made to suffer? They are pacifists and Union sympathizers, and already targeted by resentful Rebels and the Confederate sympathizers among their neighbors."

"It's horribly unfair, but they suffer doubly. Sheridan won't spare more than a handful of them. The rest face a harsh winter with nothing much to live on or they must leave their farms and flee in wagons with his retreating army."

"Hideous choice," Jack muttered. "If what you say is true, maybe I should join Jubal Early's *Army of the Valley* and fight to keep the devil out. But I'd be shot for desertion."

"Too little, too late, anyway. My dad said Gettysburg was a big nail in the coffin for the Confederacy."

Silence fell over Jack for a heavy moment. "Are you saying we lose?" His voice was husky.

She lifted her face and surveyed his solemn regard. It wasn't lost on her he'd said *we*. "Yes. Next April Lee surrenders to Grant at Appomattox Courthouse." Her father would be proud of her recall.

His jaw tight, Jack said nothing.

Should she offer her condolences, comment on the inevitability of defeat, or try and persuade him it was really for the best to preserve the Union? She could tell him the slaves were freed. He'd appreciate that…

It was difficult to determine what might be best to say. She'd heard of psychics intervening with Civil War ghosts, telling them the war was over and to move on. But what of a man as deeply invested and torn as Jack was?

"The South fought hard with much courage," she attempted.

He gave a short bitter laugh. "I experienced the

hard fighting and bravery firsthand, and some might accuse me of cowardice now, but that's not why I left. After Gettysburg, I figured the end wouldn't come in a blaze of triumph."

"No." She didn't know what else to add.

"Strange to be flat-out told, though," he muttered.

She lifted her shoulder and let it drop. "How else?"

"Indeed. Might as well spit it out."

Tilting his head at her, he weighed her with those penetrating eyes. If any part of her were lying, he'd know it. But she wasn't.

He seemed satisfied and the intensity in his gaze diminished. "You are telling me Sheridan is on the warpath and we are sitting ducks?"

"In a big bad way. But it might not be too late to help the Wengers." Surely, some parts of history could be altered.

He sighed with the weariness of a man who had slogged through endless battles. "I will ponder these fearful tidings and learn what I can of Union movements in the valley."

Visions of flames devouring all that these good people possessed in the world filled her mind. "Please do, but don't take long. There's little time." She grasped at ideas. "Think of the worst you can imagine and magnify it tenfold."

"Evie, I swear you sound like an Old Testament prophet warning of the destruction of Jerusalem."

"I kind of feel like one. The alarm needn't come from me, Jack, but urge the family to hide their food, everything they can, where it won't be found. Maybe they could dig holes outside, or tunnel back into the cellar with a pickaxe or layer branches over stuff among the trees. Find a cave the outsiders won't know of. All those things. Every bit they save counts. Winter will be brutal."

"How many soldiers are coming?" he asked quietly.

"Thousands. Like locusts covering the ground, scorching and devouring. The gates of Hell are opening."

Chapter Five

A rap on the side of the open door snared Jack's attention. He'd vaguely noted footfalls on the steps and in the hall but was too distracted by Evie's dire warning to take heed. Turning with her, he was greeted by the sight of the seven sisters and their triumphant mother. Each girl carried a bucket of water with steam rising from it. The wooden tub rode in Mary's grip. They must have dipped into the rain barrel on the back stoop and fired up the big cast-iron stove in the kitchen. No doubt, he was the intended target of their quest.

The feminine assembly in the doorway wrenched him from the dreadful tidings he struggled to comprehend. Tentative plans to cope with the crisis Evie declared nearly upon them halted. This sight was more immediately alarming.

How was he to bathe with his 'bride' in the chamber and protect her modesty, or retain a shred of dignity? Respectable men did not parade naked before ladies, but this particular lady was his presumed wife.

'Wash yourselves, make yourselves clean,' he'd heard Mary quote from the Bible, *Isaiah* something, she'd said. 'Cleanliness is next to godliness' was another of her favorites. The woman was a stickler for tidiness, and the militant set of her jaw alerted him to the near religious zeal of her mission. She was determined to see him spanking clean for his cherished bride on their wedding night.

The girls she'd recruited to her cause wore shy conspiratorial smiles. Only the eldest, Hettie, seemed distinctly ill-at-ease. She skittered away from his arched glance with pink cheeks and an apologetic shrug.

He surveyed Evie's dumbfounded expression. She seemed struck mute once more, not that he blamed her He wouldn't be surprised if she went into a dead faint But the twitch at her lips eased his conscience slightly. Unfolding circumstances must strike her as amusing, at least a little.

Unequal to opposing the formidable Mary, he smiled wryly at his *wife* of the past hour and addressed the host of females. "Ladies, how thoughtful."

"*Ya*," Mary grunted, not in the least bit fooled.

He guessed the shrewd female had discerned his reluctance. She probably considered him a pig when it came to cleanliness. Living alone in the woods made laundry and washing a challenge. In his defense, he made use of the creek flowing by his place, though not often enough for her lofty standards.

The petite figure dressed in black marched into the room and set the tub on the brown and tan striped rag rug in the center of the floor. Each sister stepped forward to empty their bucket into the wooden recess. The sweetness of marjoram rose in the steam, one of many dried herbs in the house.

"Fetch the linens, Hettie." Her mother faced Jack squarely as the girl darted away. "We are giving you the lend of one of Paul's clean shirts, a fresh pair of his drawers, socks, and undershirt. Leave us yours to wash." She raised her hand to halt his attempt at gratitude. "This is good. *Ya*?"

The tilt of her jaw dared him to refuse. He understood she was repaying him for getting her sons to safety, in her own way. But this family had saved his life when he'd had fever. He knew the resolute woman would brook no argument.

"Yes. I will leave everything outside the door for you to launder," he agreed, wondering how in the world he was to maintain any sort of decency with Evie present.

The matron of the family nodded her satisfaction, and the girls exchanged glances. Mary rounded on them, briskly clapping her hands. "Off with you. We shall return with food for you and your new bride, Jack." She gestured admittance through the petticoat ranks to Hettie whose arms were filled with the promised articles of clothing and linen towels. She set them on a chair. "Where's the soap?" her mother pounced.

The blushing young woman hastened from the room and down the hall. She returned with a blue crock containing soft brown soap scented with wintergreen, from the fragrant leaves of the woodland plant. This was Mary's personal recipe.

"Here." Her gaze downcast, Hettie set it on the washstand.

"Thank you." He suspected part of Hettie's reluctance stemmed from her partiality for him.

He found the girl attractive but hadn't considered pursuing courtship with her. For one thing he wasn't Mennonite and had no intention of converting, if that were wanted. More importantly, he couldn't offer her stability. What kind of life could he provide a young wife?

For that matter, what could he offer Evie? He slid his gaze at her, considering what he was undertaking. He'd committed himself to her protection, and if her predictions were true, hellfire would soon scorch this lush land at the hand of the Union troops advancing into the valley. With this awareness came the inherent knowledge that he still considered the Boys in Blue his enemy, while also being at odds with the Confederates.

Mostly, he just hated this wretched war. Secession had been a terrible costly mistake and matters were about to get a whole lot worse. If Rebel General Jubal Early and his *Army of the Valley* failed to keep Sheridan at bay, the countryside would swarm with Billy Yank and his flaming swords. Doubtless, unscrupulous men on either side would take advantage of an undefended populace. The chaos of war brought out the worst in those without scruples.

He couldn't focus on that right now, though. Not with Evie so near, and him soon to be as bare as the day he was born. *Dear God in heaven above.* How had he landed in this predicament?

"Come, girls." Mary intruded on his rattled thoughts, shepherding her daughters from the room. "We will bring refreshments," she added over her shoulder. "Shut the door behind us and open when you are ready for your supper."

"I will. Thanks again, ma'am." He answered automatically, like a soldier on drill. When the line of skirts vanished from sight, he turned to Evie with a low groan, weighing the mix of undeniable humor and gaping surprise in her face. "My apologies. You must be flabbergasted."

"Not entirely. I mean, well, yes. A lot. But it's not

your fault," she stammered.

"No. I didn't foresee this circumstance. Best avert your gaze, dear lady," he cautioned with a slight smile. "Be it on your head if you peek and I offend your delicate sensibilities."

"My what?" Giggling, she sank onto the bed in a lacy puff of skirts and petticoats. "You really are a gentleman."

He straightened his shoulders. "I trust I am."

"Without question. And don't worry. I won't look but doubt I would be offended if I did. Not by you."

Her praise and the glow in her eyes warmed him. "I shall take that as a compliment."

"Do. You're the handsomest husband I've ever had."

"Have you had others?" he teased, walking across the room to the door.

"Not that I recall, but if I had, you would be streaks ahead of any. I've never known a man like you."

The wistfulness in her tone washed over him in a tide of hope. "I pray you never do." He found he meant every word.

"I wouldn't be foolish enough to seek a duplicate with the original right in front of me."

Her clever phrasing and the intent behind her assertion buoyed him. Maybe he was mad, but he ardently wished this most unlikely of all women might share a future with him.

"You wouldn't find another like me even if you sought one. I'm alone in no man's land."

"Then we must find a way to be together." Her voice was little more than a whisper.

Had he heard her rightly? He shut the door and

pivoted, searching her eyes by candlelight. Gone, any humor in their blue-gray depths. Sincerity shone back at him.

God help him, she had the face of an angel, a tantalizing woman-child unlike any he'd ever met before or ever would again. He stood lost in wonder. The wash of moonbeams slanting through the window bathed her in a pearly sheen, her lacy pink shawl resembling the inside of a polished shell.

Her presence enriched the plain room like a vibrant jewel, and he felt as if he had a claim to her, not only because of the pretended marriage, but because she belonged to him. It was as if they had been together before, but he couldn't think when. He had nothing to base the strong sensation on except emotion. If only she truly were his.

Speak now, or forever hold your peace, he told himself. "Yes. I believe we must find a way." His voice was husky with an entirely different emotion than the aching regret that pervaded his mood before.

Her eyes glistered. "Do you really mean it?"

Could he show her just how much he meant it, how fast he was succumbing to her charms? Did he dare proceed? If he aligned himself with her, there would be no return.

He had the war and his duty to think of. But he and she might have little time left before the invaders came and the countryside was overrun. If he were caught, he'd be taken prisoner, or shot—by either side. This could be his sole opportunity to act.

"Jack?"

At the soft plea hovering in his name, he strode across the room and scooped her up from the bed. He gathered her in his arms, inhaling her flowery perfume, her hair spilling over them both. Desire rushed through him like a scorching gale. The coming inferno she warned of enflamed him and he clasped her closer still. She tilted her face toward his, her eyes drifting shut, lashes brushing her cheeks, and he bent his head, covering her lips with his rapturous mouth.

Perfection, two beings coming together at the exact moment preordained for them. Flames consumed him as he slowly circled with her in his embrace, kissing her all the while. A drum beat in his heart, an ancient song known to all men tumbling in love. He had climbed mountains with less hammering inside, and her chest rose and fell against his.

If lips could speak without words, he conveyed his fast-growing devotion in a torrent. She returned the heated pressure on her mouth, her slender arms entwined around his neck. Everything he'd ever wanted or cared about, seemed as nothing compared to this moment with her. Headwaters crashing together and swirling him away, could have no greater effect.

How had he lived before Evie? How could he ever bear to let her go?

Impossible. Unthinkable. He scarcely knew her, and yet, he did.

Breaking for breath, he pressed his lips to her satiny neck, eliciting tiny shivers in her, furthering his delight. "Will you marry me and truly be Mrs. Jack Ramsey?"

"Yes." She didn't hesitate, her panted reply beyond belief.

Was any of this real? Maybe he was delirious, out of his head, wandering in a fevered dream of piercing joy. "I don't know how we shall live," he added, reclaiming her pliant lips.

"We'll manage somehow," she said, in between the sweetest, most fervent kisses he'd ever experienced. "Here or there…" she trailed off.

"By *there*, you mean the future in this house with your grandmother?" he clarified, doubtful she'd surrendered that fantasy since entering the chamber she'd proclaimed her own.

"Yes. Grandma G. wants me to help her run the farm, and she'd be wild about you. In fact, if you were there with me I would willingly stay—"

He disrupted her touching avowal, silencing her with a tender kiss. Moments passed, their lips conveying what could not be defined in words, because it made no earthly sense. Their hearts hammered. He swore he felt hers beating, too. How long he stood cradling her, he didn't know. Footsteps in the hall reminded him the family awaited the couple's readiness for their wedding supper. For that, he must climb into the tub, and emerge freshly scrubbed, scented with wintergreen, and wearing the borrowed clothes.

"They're waiting." Breaking from Evie with a sigh, he reluctantly lowered her to the bed. "Duty calls. I would love to *discuss* my intentions further with you, but I've got my marching orders. Better get on with my bath."

She gazed up at him in lip-twitching amusement, appearing more desirable than ever. "You mean, you are going to strip off your clothes now, and I'm to stay here?" Bubbly laughter escaped her.

"That's the plan." He strode to the chair and positioned it near the tub.

Shaking his head at the craziness of this undertaking, he slid the strap of his black canvas haversack from his shoulder and slung the supply pouch over the high back.

"And I'm not to look because you're guarding my modesty?" she continued.

"Correct." He might as well have said 'bizarre' because it was.

Instead, he removed his brown jacket and hung it beside the haversack, unbuttoned his butternut-colored vest and added it to the growing collection. His gray suspenders joined the rest, and he pulled his once white shirt off over his head. The undershirt followed, both crumpling at his feet.

He met Evie's admiring gaze, and it wasn't lost on him that her eyes wandered over his bare chest. A tinge of rose pinkened her smooth cheeks, which suited him just fine. His gaze had wandered plenty over her curves since he first saw her.

"Final warning." He grinned and pulled off his chestnut-colored riding boots, standing them on the floor. "My trousers are coming off next."

Mary hadn't requested these or his vest and jacket for the laundry, nor was he parting with them. In critical times like this, a man must be prepared to dress and act in an instant. He unbuckled his leather belt and laid it and the holstered revolver over the chair, then unbuttoned his fly and let the trousers slide to his ankles. He stepped out and added that vital article to the others.

If Evie watched him, the most he could do to guard what little propriety remained was to keep his backside toward her. With this in mind, he lowered his drawers and heaped them on the wash pile. His socks followed. Snatching a towel from the stack of clean linens on the chair, he clutched it around him. The linen didn't cover nearly enough. Mostly his front. He climbed into the water and draped the towel along the side in readiness.

"Pretend I'm not here." He sank farther down into the still warm liquid.

Doggone it. He'd forgotten the soap on the washstand. Shadows partly hid him, and the water he soaked in was a dark pool. Maybe she could help him without causing too much offense.

"Except, would you mind passing me that blue crock?" he asked his silent companion.

Had she peeked, was she scandalized?

"If you can do so in all modesty," he added, burning with curiosity as to her reaction, but he faced the door and could not see her expression. He glanced over his shoulder.

"Think I can manage." She gathered her skirts and walked to the stand. Lifting the crock, she tiptoed to his side, as if this better preserved her decorum. With her face carefully averted, she extended the container to him.

He took it from her. "I also need the pitcher for rinsing." He hadn't planned this watery assault very well, possibly because he was in the chamber with the beautiful woman he'd embraced and proposed to only moments ago.

"It's full of water, too." She retrieved the vessel and passed that to him. "Shall I climb in there with you?"

He met the mirth in her eyes. "You vixen. You peeked."

She nodded, puckering her lips to suppress a grin. "Only for a second," she reasoned, as if that didn't count.

A smile tugged at his mouth. "Still want to marry me?"

"Even more."

She bowled him over. Utterly. He pointed dripping fingers at the bed. "Go. Wait at a respectable distance," he insisted, muffling the laughter rising in his throat.

"Yes. All right." Snatching the pitcher from him, she poured cold water over his head.

"Scamp," he sputtered.

"A little." She erupted in giggles and set the pitcher by the tub, darting across the room in a flurry of skirts.

He needn't have worried about her fainting at the sight of a man without apparel. She had more spirit than he'd realized, a sustaining attribute they might well need.

Not might. Would. And she was very young. He felt ancient by comparison. More than a few years stretched between them when it came to experience. He never wanted her to see the carnage he'd witnessed.

How was he to fight in a war he wanted no part of, and shield her from the mayhem at the same time? Because the hour was coming when he must choose a side, and the only one that struck a chord within him was Virginia and his beloved valley.

Chapter Six

"Wake up, Evie." The familiar voice whispered near her ear, while a firm hand clasped her shoulder and gave her a shake. "Wake up," the woman urged, the sweet spiciness of rose, jasmine, and vanilla perfume wafting from her. "We don't have much time."

What? Why? Jolted from a deep sleep, Evie blinked heavy eyes and focused drowsily on the dimly seen figure bent beside her bed—technically the Wengers' bed.

She recognized the woman in the long white nightgown, a lady's outfit, or two, draped over her arm. "Grandma G.?"

"Yes, dear child."

What was she doing here? Had Evie returned to the present?

Fear rifled through her. What of Jack? She couldn't be parted from him again.

Again? The odd insistence echoed in her frazzled mind as she sat bolt upright in her chemise. "Where am I?"

"In between times. The house is warbling," her eccentric relation whispered.

"It's *what*?" Evie couldn't see straight under the weight of grogginess, let alone think clearly. Where did that leave Jack? Was he still beside her?

Panic flooded her, and she swiveled toward the

space on her right. Darkness swallowed the spot. She desperately patted the place where he'd been, seeking his solid warmth. *Empty.*

Wait. Hazy memory returned of him vowing he would bunk on the cot to preserve what was left of her modesty and not put temptation in their path. Too drowsy to argue the point, she'd only requested he stay with her awhile, and must have fallen asleep almost instantly. Was he over there?

With the intensity of a Border collie, she trained her gaze on the narrow cot along the pale wall beyond the washstand. The milky stream of moonlight slanting through the window revealed the outline of his slumbering form tucked beneath a blanket. Her chest thudded in gratitude.

"Oh, thank God." She muffled her outburst so as not to disrupt his few hours of rest and pointed shakily at him. "That's Jack Ramsey, Grandma, former Confederate officer, and guide for the Unionist Underground Railroad. He's also my pretend husband and real fiancée. It all happened very fast." Her head still spun from the intensity of their meeting.

She expected a snort or shock at her bold declaration regarding a perfect stranger, but the unflappable Gladys McIntyre didn't seem overly surprised. "I thought you two might find each other again."

Evie gaped at her; that odd word choice had surfaced once more. "Are Jack and I acquainted?"

"Yes. Very much so."

"But that makes no sense," she hissed.

"You are from the past, sweet girl." Grandma G. shifted the heaped clothes into her arms, adding a pair of black boots. "The house has wanted to take you back. The timing had to be right."

Mystified, she clutched the pile of fabric and footwear, letting this inexplicable revelation sink in. "I suppose the house must want me here, but it's awfully weird to speak of the place as if it has goals."

"In a way, it has." Grandma G. passed her the hat she wore for riding, and a stylish bonnet—trendy for the nineteenth century, anyway. "Houses absorb emotions whether good or bad from those who have lived in them, and sometimes retain a ghost or two."

Now the woman was speaking of spirits? Evie grappled with her strange philosophy. "I suppose that makes sense, as much as anything." She'd heard weirder stuff from space alien devotees. "What of you? How did you get through to the past?"

The hurried female picked up a vaguely familiar carpet bag, like a small suitcase made from a flowery wine-colored rug. She set it on the end of the bed. "Like I said, the house is fading back and forth between the present day and the era you find yourself in. I'm not sure what the term for this changeable phenomenon is. I call it a warble in time, or warbling. You have remained in eighteen sixty-four. I've popped in for a visit."

Her jaw sagging, she stared at her grandmother's indistinct features. "Will I stay here forever?"

"I surely hope not," Grandma G. said under breath. "Your family would be most upset. If there is any danger of that, I will find a way to fetch you back. Take care, child, and return to the present with Jack at your earliest opportunity."

"When will that be? Are you certain he can come?" Baffled beyond words, she wondered if her grandmother was some sort of witch.

"You'll know when to act," the indomitable Gladys assured her in a whisper. "Instinct will prompt you. And yes, Jack must go, too. But he probably won't agree until the last possible moment. For that matter, the house won't let you return until then. It has a reason for transporting you when it did."

She spoke matter-of-factly, while Evie was floored.

Grandma G. gave her shoulder a reassuring pat, and smoothed the cloth heaped in her lap. "I've brought your green riding habit, and the checked day dress, plus your cloak, some toiletries, accessories, and lots of snacks. That sort of thing." She indicated the carpet bag. "You'll see. This should help ease your stay here. You didn't have a chance to pack."

"Not hardly," Evie muttered.

"Good thing you were wearing your Victorian gown when you traveled back," the enthusiast continued. "Though that one's a bit dressy for this time and place."

"Rather." The Wengers must wonder at her extravagance in wartime when many wore black, the hue of mourning. "Thanks for the things you brought. I don't understand what's happening," she faltered. "Everything feels like a dream."

"No doubt. Oh, look. There it goes again." The knowledgeable woman gestured at the walls, drawing Evie's scattered attention to the strange phenomena.

She glimpsed her décor from twenty-eighteen as if through a wavering bubble stretching the height and width of the room. She reached out and touched her bedside lamp, and the covering on the bed was her own quilt. Then the bubble reversed, and the room appeared as it did in the Wenger's day. The house was altering between past and present in what her grandmother termed the *warble* effect.

Odd, Evie hadn't noticed her surroundings switching in and out of eras before. Was she that unobservant?

"How often does it do this?" she asked.

"Now and then. I sometimes find myself in the past. I've been in the Wenger's kitchen more than once." Grandma G. paused, her manner deeply thoughtful. "Such a nice family. Of course, that was years ago."

Evie startled. "Who did they think you were?"

"A kindly woman passing by, on the occasions they saw me. They didn't always. And I've been further back in time than them. The house is kind of like a volcano, quiet for a long stretch, and then active. It's warbling a lot tonight. I realized at once when I got up to go to the bathroom. That's when I checked on you and saw you going in and out of eras. So, I packed the bag, gathered your stuff, and stepped through."

"I see," Evie said, but she didn't. Not remotely. Who would have the presence of mind to pack? "The whispers aren't here now."

"No. They emanate from this period in the house." Grandma G. gave her a reassuring pat. "The window of opportunity may soon close. I must get back to my own time. When I step through the bedroom door I will be transported forward."

"Wait." Evie caught her sleeve. "Why did you say I'm from the past?" She hadn't ventured here before now.

The plump figure hesitated as if uncertain whether

to answer, her expression hidden. "I suppose you should know... Ages ago, in the mid eighteenth century, a young married couple named Joseph and Hannah Gruber built the log cabin at the heart of this house. The French and Indian War broke out soon after. Sadly, neither of them survived it."

"What?" Evie gulped. "You mean, they were killed?"

"Joseph was. A passing war party shot him while he was out plowing. No one knew which tribe attacked."

The news struck Evie hard for a man slain so long ago. "Did it matter which Indians did the killing?"

"Yes, if you wanted to recover a captive," her sensible grandmother replied. "Warriors took Hannah with them."

"Poor girl." She envisioned the weight of grief the young widow must have born.

"Yes, and bear in mind, Hannah and Joseph were Mennonite Pacifists," the storyteller continued. "Men in their community are forbidden to fight and would have had to try and purchase her freedom, eventually."

Evie imagined weeks dragging into months and years. "That might never happen."

"And often didn't," the narrator agreed. "One of your female ancestors never came home. But in this event, armed men from a nearby fort recovered Hannah and several other captives before the war party got far. The poor girl didn't last long upon her return. Died from fever and a broken heart. The pair are buried together in the tiny graveyard behind the house, beside the big oak at the back of the meadow. You remember?"

Stunned, Evie simply nodded. The site was regarded as sacred. Now she knew why.

"But Hannah and Joseph's tragic tale doesn't end there. Both were reborn," Grandma G. added in hushed tones "One in the nineteenth century and the other in the twenty-first. I will let you guess which is which."

Evie stared at the dimly seen face. "How can you possibly know this?"

She heaved a sigh. "Because I've seen the past and read accounts in old journals and letters. And I have a sixth sense about these things. I just don't always say."

"That's the understatement of the century, whichever one we're in." Normally, the woman was as tightlipped as a clam when it came to sharing profundities, and now this bombshell?

"You wouldn't have believed me even if I had told you sooner," Grandma G. gently reminded her.

"You've got that right. I have no memory of Joseph and Hannah or these earlier times."

"The house has and is offering you a second chance, child. Somewhere inside, you are instinctively drawn to this place, despite your fears. That's why Jack can't keep away. There's something else you must know. Jack Ramsey doesn't survive this war either. Get him to the future before the house is ablaze."

Evie's chest tightened under the pressing weight of this black disclosure, and the hammering returned. "How do I do that? When does The Burning begin, exactly?"

"September twenty-sixth. This farm wasn't set on fire until early October. I'm not sure of the exact day, but looting was widespread before then."

"You said the house was partly saved?" She

snatched at the gleam of hope.

"Yes. As soon as the burning party rode off, the family rushed to put out the fire before the entire structure was consumed. And it rained, so that helped."

Grandma. G. gestured at the wavering room. "This may be the final warble in a while. I better scoot. Oh, and Evie, when in doubt, pray." She brushed a kiss to her cold cheek and darted away at a fast clip for a woman of her size. She wasn't kidding about the need to move. Her white-clad figure disappeared the instant she stepped out the door; it shut behind her as if of its own accord.

Thoughts scattered through Evie's mind like startled geese in heavy mist. Laden with cloth, she sat staring at the cot where Jack lay unaware of these strange tidings and events. It seemed her lot in life to convey weird happenings to him. She couldn't deny she'd seen the past melding with the present, but still hardly believed her eyes.

Whether or not she had any memory of the tragic plight of the eighteenth-century couple, she sensed the truth of her grandmother's assertion. The woman spoke with quiet authority and had no reason to make it up, plus Evie had seen the gravestones. The names were faded, but Hannah and Joseph were chiseled deep. Someone, their families, she guessed, had loved the pair dearly to bury them with such care and sorrow. Their pain seeped into the very earth.

Now, here she was, trying to keep Jack alive and get him to the future before he perished, again, in another war.

She'd always sensed Grandma G. knew more than she let on, but dear God. How was Evie to grasp these stunning revelations, let alone convince Jack?

It was true, she had agreed to stay at the house despite her fears, and Jack was attached to the home and the Wenger family. This place had a hold on them both. With Mennonites in his earlier life and his draw to them in his present one, it was no wonder he was torn between fighting for Virginia and the Confederacy and not taking lives at all. He also abhorred slavery, as did the plain people.

Did Evie and Jack's distant ties to each other account for the instant attraction between them?

Maybe...she couldn't explain it any other way.

She still didn't know the chronology of events regarding his fate in this era, but it had to do with Sheridan and The Burning. Surely, Jack wouldn't remain in the home after it was set afire? That would be insane, and he was smart. Street-smart, she supposed, in the rural sense. Whatever cleverness was attached to secretive country guides fit him.

By heaven, she was determined to prevent his untimely end and get him to the future.

But would he want to go? And leave everything he knew behind?

She sensed a vibrancy in the past that beat standing in line at Wally World, and much of contemporary life. But she didn't doubt this era held trials and dangers that would dampen her ardor and make her long for modern amenities. Though she doubted anything could lessen her preoccupation with Jack Ramsey.

Chapter Seven

Sounds of the farmstead rousing to wakefulness seeped into Jack's muzzy consciousness. Bird song mixed with the crowing roosters. One cockerel had announced the dawn since the wee hours, its crow punctuated his dreams. He tuned his ear to hens clucking in the yard outside the bedroom window. Pigs grunted in their sty, cows bawled for their breakfast, and the high-pitched bleat of sheep carried from the distant meadow. The earthy scent of animals drifted inside along with the tangy aroma of hickory smoke from the kitchen hearth.

Ah, yes. He remembered falling asleep on the Wengers' cot, a thrill darting through him as he envisioned his fair new wife/fiancé slumbering in the nearby bed. Then he recalled they shared the chamber she'd claimed was hers in the future, and he stifled a groan. The day was too early for these confounding thoughts, he argued with himself, but they rapidly returned.

He mused drowsily on the wondrous, baffling young woman he'd encountered last evening and committed himself to in the blink of an eye. Evie seemed in earnest regarding her assertions of another life lived in this house. By all appearances, she was sincere.

How had she come by these peculiar notions? She

must have *the sight* to know all she had professed about the war, but this gift couldn't fully account for her bizarre claims. Much required an explanation he had none for, except madness.

She didn't strike him as a lunatic, and he'd known a few, nor was she a liar. He'd read the sincerity in her eyes. The only remaining possibility was that she had spoken the truth, the strangest option imaginable, but he'd ruled out the other choices.

He must be hopelessly muddled to consider the plausibility of her assertion. *Damn, he needed coffee.*

He'd do handstands and shout *hurrah* if the dad-blame Union blockade cutting off supplies to Southern ports ran aground and the black brew were speedily restored. Meager substitutes of roasted chicory root, parched corn, or dried beets did nothing to sharpen his wits. He might better understand the fascinating, perplexing creature that was Evie after several bracing cups of the robust drink everyone in Dixie longed for, while Northerners craved Southern tobacco. Let them have it. He didn't smoke, but badly missed coffee.

It astonished him to think he hadn't even known the girl for twelve hours. And yet, the bond between them seemed to extend much farther back into the misty recesses of time. From the first moment he saw her, something inside him had quickened and he knew his life would never again be the same. Part of him feared she was the stuff of dreams, a fantasy woman he'd conjured out of his aching loneliness.

Please Lord, no. His gut knotted at the bleak thought.

Jolted fully awake, he sat up in the borrowed white shirt and homed in on Evie's corner of the room. *There*.

Relief rolled through him.

The muted glow coming through the window revealed her seated upright in bed, a shawl around her shoulders to ward off the chill air. Autumn was upon them, the weather showing signs of the coming change, and her honey-streaked brown hair spilled over her like a second mantle. Seemingly lost in reverie, she stared straight ahead.

What a rare vision to be greeted by first thing in the morning, or anytime. Normally, he was alone, or in the company of gamey men.

Dragging his eyes from her, he explored the clothes heaped in her lap. Where had all that come from?

A hat and bonnet? He hadn't noted these last evening. Her head was bare. Did he spy a riding crop? Boots?

"Evie." Reluctant to be overheard by any of the family, he summoned her in a whisper. "What in the world?"

She turned toward him, her face ghostly in the silvery light. "You're awake."

"I presume." Part of him wondered if he were still asleep.

Her answering smile shimmered through him. He wanted nothing more than to tumble with her in his arms and kiss her, but he must think. Brushing back lengths of freshly washed hair, he swept a hand at her. "Where did you get all of this?" He slid his disbelieving gaze the length of her mattress. "Is that a carpet bag?"

"*Yessirree*," she said softly. "My grandmother visited in the night and brought me this stuff." She spoke as if the woman had simply stepped in from the next room.

"When? I must have been dead to the world." If he'd been on sentry duty, he would have been shot.

"You were sound asleep, but we kept our voices down so as not to wake you," she confided in equally muted tones.

"Most considerate." He couldn't believe this conversation, or the goods heaped on and about her.

"Apparently, I should always carry a bag with me in the event I'm zapped back in time before I get a chance to pack." She spoke as if this were a normal discussion.

"It looks as if a peddler upended his pack on you. And a seamstress paid a call, as well, while I slumbered."

"There's a reason for that." Evie drew a breath. "Grandma G. came through a window in time, she called it a warble, and returned the same way. There," she finished, exhaling.

He gave a low whistle. "Tarnation, woman. You are the strangest girl."

"Yes," she agreed without a hitch. "I've reached the same conclusion."

A wry smile tugged at his lips while wonder sparked inside him. "I must admit, these strange goings on are not of your making. That carpet bag didn't waltz in here on its own, and you couldn't have gotten it or that mountain of stuff by yourself during the night."

"No. I couldn't have." She slanted her gaze at him, challenge in her face. "Maybe you should start believing me, even if all of this is too weird for words."

"Maybe I should." He exhaled again, wondering how he was to accept such incomprehensible logic?

He was a rational man. Normally, and reason

would be expected of them.

"What do we tell the Wengers about your newly acquired goods, or will you explain the visit from a grandmother who resides in the future?"

"No. That's too farfetched. Although, Grandma G. told me she's met them on several occasions."

"Of course, she did," he muttered, struggling to grasp the crazy reality that accompanied Evie.

She gestured for his attention. "Here's a thought. What if we say my things were left on the porch last night and we forgot during the excitement of meeting everyone, then you slipped back downstairs and got them for me later?"

He shrugged a half-hearted affirmation of her plan. "If we're spinning yarns, that one is as good as any. But it's a big carpet bag for us to have hauled on horseback, seeing as Buck must have carried us both. Plus, you have more clothes than it, alone, accounts for."

"True." She paused for a pensive moment. "What if I had my own mount? We could say we tied the bag on behind, and a roll of my clothes."

"Sure. Spin away, as we're making up everything anyway, though I think you would need a trunk for your wardrobe. Where did you get this phantom horse?" He hadn't given it to her.

"Oh, I already have one in the future. Well, Grandma G. owns several, but I ride when I like. There's a gold Palomino mare with excellent manners named Honey Lemon and a roan gelding who clips the sky when he jumps called *Fast*. And a lovely pair of matched thoroughbreds that pull the carriage. Visitors go for rides and have their pictures taken, often with me. A guy comes in, I guess you'd call him a groom, who cares for the horses and drives the carriage."

"Certainly." Jack rubbed his clean-shaven chin while digesting this information, much of it washing over him. Visions of a fine carriage and prancing mounts danced through his head. "I'm sure your grandmother's horses are among the best. How do you propose to fetch one back from the future?"

"I'm not sure," she allowed.

"Even if you found a way, any animal that splendid would immediately be stolen unless we hid it well.

"That's it." She clapped her hands together. "We can say Honey Lemon was left in the woods with your horse and the others and was taken or wandered off...some unfortunate occurrence."

"Highly likely, were it true."

"It soon will be with Sheridan coming," she reminded him.

The black warning darkened his mood. "I must ride out this morning and discover whatever I can about his movements."

"Not without me." She lifted her chin. "I'm coming, too."

"Women do not ride about with rebel guerillas on the prowl. Some are up to a lot of no good, and the men will gladly take shots at me. It's doubly dangerous for you in my company."

Insistence lit her eyes, like twin flames. "Maybe not as much if I ride with you. Unless they shoot women?"

"Not routinely."

"Well, then. Take me along and let's see what we can learn of Sheridan, while I rack my brains to recall what I've been told. Grandma G. packed my riding habit for a reason."

"Does she possess the sight, too?" Perhaps this inclination ran in Evie's blood.

"I expect so. I'm not sure I have this ability in the way you think, but I feel it's crucial I go with you."

Plainly, Evie was determined, and had mastered being both maddening and adorable in one, probably drove her grandmother to distraction. If he did as she wished, he might get them both killed. On the other hand, she'd put any man they met, soldier, civilian, guerilla, even Sheridan himself, off his guard. And this would give Jack a chance to act or negotiate.

He loosed a weighty sigh. "Are you always this stubborn?"

"Yes. One of my finer qualities. It gets worse."

"That so?" He snorted. "I can see it now. We're out riding when a fellow asks your maiden name. You answer, and he says, 'McIntyre? Any relation to Lucas with the Fourteenth Virginia?' and you say, 'he's my great-great grandfather.' "

The grin she gave Jack further charmed him. "It's four greats back and his first name was George. He lives in Augusta County." She tapped a finger beneath her chin. "Odd to think."

"Indeed. Good heavens, girl, where are you from?"

"Twenty Eighteen."

She could have knocked him over with a feather, he was so walloped by surprise. He did some quick figuring. "That's more than one hundred and fifty years from now."

"I know." She seemed to have come to terms with the gulf between the dates and wasn't flummoxed as he was. "I mentioned the years last night," she reminded him.

What could he say? "I thought you were addlepated."

"Not in this regard." She gazed toward the door. "Now, where is the bathroom in this version of my house?"

"*Your* house?"

"Well, it will be one day if Grandma G. has her way. She's also hardheaded, I should mention. My family is."

"No doubt." He shook his head, bemused, baffled, and beguiled. "There's a chamber pot under your bed, or you may visit the privy near the garden."

She wrinkled her nose. "Let's dress, with our eyes averted, of course, then you can escort me to the outhouse. I suppose it's like camping. Not that I like camping much. I hope Grandma G. packed toilet paper."

He arched his brows at her. "What?"

"You'll see. I'll look." She set the pile of clothes aside and crawled the length of the bed in her shift and shawl. Long hair brushing the coverlet, she snagged the carpet bag, opened it, and peered inside. The light beyond the window had brightened and revealed the treasures within.

"Thank heavens." She held up rolls of white paper. "Here it is. For use in the privy. Grandma G. packed a case of toiletries and fresh underclothes. Oh, good. She remembered the coffee."

Instantly alert, he riveted his gaze on the bag. The heck with having Evie avert her gaze—she'd already snuck a peek at him wearing far less. He sprang to his feet, aware of her startled expression, and snatched his trousers from the back of the chair. He pulled them on over the clean drawers he'd worn overnight, tucked in his shirt, buttoned the fly, and bounded across the room and into bed beside her.

"Show me," he invited. "I haven't had any coffee since the last swap with Billy Yank. I swear if soldiers on either side could put their heads together, we would conclude this war in thirty minutes, after swapping to our heart's content."

"Probably so." Slightly flustered, likely from his brash behavior, she lifted a red paper bag labeled *Coffee*. It looked as if it held a pound of the roasted beans.

A delectable whiff caught his nose, and he inhaled. "Divine."

"You'll love the future, Jack, if I can get you there. All the coffee you could possibly want awaits you."

"I can want a lot." The idea of traveling to some distant realm with his dream girl was beyond him. *This* was real, he thought, breathing deeply.

She waved an intriguing jar. "There's also instant coffee."

He was in awe. "Like Christmas morn, only a heap better than the past three dismal celebrations." He eyed the glass container, filled with dark brown grounds. At least, that's what he assumed they were. "How do you prepare this brew?"

"Stir a spoonful into boiling water to make a cup. Drink it black or add cream and sugar. Grandma G. included small containers of both packaged individually."

"In there? What a marvel," he breathed out.

"I suppose so, if you've never seen it before. She

was in a hurry so didn't stop to find suitable wrappings to pack the stuff in. You can tell it's not from this time period."

Jack gave Evie a look. "You're in the *South* in wartime. We don't have much of anything no matter what you wrap it in."

"True. I'm desperately trying to remember my history."

He drew his brows together. "How odd to hear this day described as history, as if we are naught but dust and bones. Even if you are from another age, life is happening here right now, and it's every bit as important to the people living it as your future world is to you."

"I know. Sorry," she offered, but he doubted she began to grasp what it meant to dwell in this time and place.

She continued rummaging through the carpet bag. "Granola bars!" She opened a narrow colorful box and took out a rectangular shape, about the length of her hand.

The crinkly colorful packaging was unfamiliar. "To eat?"

"Yes. And loaded with energy. We can keep going a while on one of these. I've seen shows about survival," she told him. "Like plays, with moving images."

"Whatever that is, I agree, survival is essential."

"And this will help." She tore at the wrapping and pulled out the contents. "Here. Take a bite."

He'd undoubtedly tasted worse, if this bar thing turned out to be vile. No maggots crawled in it like some of the hard tack he'd had. A welcome sign.

Unsure what to expect, he bit into a crunchy confection of oats, dried fruit, nuts, and honey. "Delicious." He refrained from devouring the entire bar and offered it to her.

She took a bite and passed it back. "Keep it, I'll get my own. There are a dozen boxes with eight bars each."

"Such abundance." He bit off more of the sweet goodness, chewing in wonder. After living off the land with his hunting skills, and breakfasts of venison or squirrel supplemented by corncakes and molasses, if he were fortunate, this was bliss. "How much food do you have in there?"

The first pale rays of sunlight played over her head as she took stock. "Umm, besides the coffee and bars, there's beef jerky, bags of nuts, pretzels, dried fruit, cookies, chocolate—"

He clasped her arm. "In truth? Chocolate is as scarce as hen's teeth."

"Not anymore. Grandma G. stashed a lot of dark chocolate bars in here. Rich stuff."

This was too much for him to grasp, while Evie took everything for granted. "Unheard of bounty. Your grandmother must be an exceedingly wealthy lady."

"No. Only comfortable," she insisted.

The word struck a discordant note in him, her usage of it provoking. He narrowed his gaze at her. "*Comfortable*? How indulged are you?"

Her eyes clouded like shadows over lake water. "What do you mean?"

He waved his hand at the room as if to encompass the house. "*Comfort* is a roof over your head, a warm bed. Food on the table. A fire in the hearth. I go weeks, sometimes months, without all but the meanest things.

What you have in that bag is more than folk in the valley can claim a fraction of."

She considered him soberly. "I didn't realize."

"No. You have no notion the wealth your grandmother has, or how fortunate you are in your situation with her. Why did you forfeit such grandeur and journey to a time destined to be the worst the valley has ever endured, if what you say comes to pass?"

A mix of tenderness, wounded pride, and determination shone back at him from her glistening gaze. "There can be only one answer. For you, Jack. It's always been you."

Her avowal knifed through him. "*Always*?"

"You and I go back much farther than this. My grandmother said we lived here together before."

He sucked in his breath. "That is the most outrageous declaration I ever heard, Evie."

Unshed tears glinted in her eyes. "I agree, and yet, I sense the truth of it."

Pondering her mindboggling assertion, he sat with her in silence. "I also sense this in my spirit," he admitted more gently. "Though not in any manner except feelings."

She entwined her fingers through his and clasped his hand. "I have no memories of us as we once were but sense a deeper connection than the one we formed so quickly last night. Jack, Grandma G. said *we* were the young couple who built this house when it was a log cabin."

A torrent of thoughts and sensations swirled inside him as he tried to comprehend the dumbfounding claim. He cherished Evie's trust and the natural way she'd taken his hand. How right she felt by his side, as if they'd always been together, and yet, parted far too soon.

This seemingly impossible connection might be a chance for them to recover what they once had, long ago. A confession hovered on his tongue, and he finally gave it voice. "What you say floods my senses, but it explains a great deal.

"Yes. It's a lot to absorb," she whispered.

He pressed her fingers to his lips. "To ponder you journeying here from another time, and us sharing a former life together?" He shook his head. "How can we understand this? Meanwhile, I fear you are not ready for what lies ahead in this place, dear lady."

She winked at tears. "No. I dare say I'm not. But I will toughen up. I must."

A vision of the war nearly at their door raised its ugly head. "That remains to be seen. I don't want to return you to your grandmother in a wooden box, supposing I even could."

Evie swallowed hard, the stubborn tilt still at her jaw. "I don't want you to, either. Come what may, though, we face it together."

He contemplated her for a long moment. "You can go with me today. Then we shall see."

She would retreat when she realized what they were up against, he felt certain, and he would do his utmost to protect her today. Then she must remain with the Wengers while he came and went, if they agreed. What else could he do?

A smile trembled at her mouth. "Do I ride with you on Buck, or can we borrow the Wenger's mare for me?"

He studied her skeptically. She was a lady, not an

officer in the bloody cavalry. "Do you really ride well enough to head out on your own mount?"

"I have the outfit, don't I?" she asked, in turn.

"And that proves your ability, does it? Many dandies possess the clothes. I thought you said your dress was for picture taking, not merit?"

Pure steel narrowed her eyes. "I can ride, Mr. Smarty Pants. Wait and see. I might leave you in the dust."

He chuckled. "Very well. Let's go straightway after breakfast. I'm not missing out on brewed coffee, and the Wengers will be thrilled to share in our wedding bounty, Mrs. Ramsey."

She tightened her hold on his fingers. "Amen to that."

He gazed at her, the shadow of a memory returning…of his sweet wife poised in the cabin doorway and her smiling eyes…Evie's eyes. They must have known another time together, and another war.

Deep inside him, realization came. They hadn't survived that conflict. Somehow, they must survive this one. He prayed God would give him a nudge regarding danger, and a lot of help.

Chapter Eight

Jack? Evie swept from the bedroom in her forest green riding habit to find her supposed husband/fiancé waiting on the landing. He stood at the window, his back to her, gazing out at the dewy garden and fields beyond.

Warmth flushed her at the sight of his lean figure, an arm pressed against the beveled glass, his blonde hair shining in the early light. He turned at her tread and smiled.

Tingles zinged through her. How handsome he was this morning, not that he hadn't been last night, but she knew him better now. The force of his appeal struck her afresh, and it was humbling that such a man should care for her. She'd never been very popular in school. Many kids labeled her weird, not that this was necessarily a bad thing. There was worse.

Granted, she was unusual, evident in the fact that she stood in the nineteenth century version of the house. But none of her former freakiness had prepared her for this adventure with Jack. Come what may, in this moment, she wouldn't trade it for anything.

The hum of voices reached her from the kitchen, the hub of the home. Lifting her skirts, she hurried to where he stood. The admiration in his eyes, like sunlight on deep woods' fern, told her he approved her attire.

"You are so beautiful." His voice hushed in near reverence. "I never saw a lady like you in these parts."

His praise thrilled her. "Staunton probably has some." She named the historic city in neighboring Augusta County.

"Well, yes. Probably so there," he agreed. "Not in the middle of farmland, only a hop, skip, and a jump away from the foothills of the Alleghenies."

Her cheeks warmed. "I know I don't fit in well here."

Smiling, he reached his hand to smooth a tendril of her hair, gathered in a loose waterfall cascading down her back. "You are a duchess compared to simple country folk. But we are aiming for diversion, and you are definitely that. I hope I can keep my wits about me with all of this *distraction*."

A ripple of pleasure ran through her. "Grandma G.'s passion for everything Victorian has come in handy."

His sandy brows arched. "What is Victorian?"

"The age we're living in now, while Queen Victoria reigns in England, which lasted a long time, by the way."

"Fine by me. Long live the queen." He waved a hand at her. "Is Victoria the reason you are dressed as you are?"

"I expect so. And I might be a fashion plate, but at least my habit fits the era. Well, *sort of*," she amended. "I'm a bit of an odd duck, as my grandmother says."

"But elegant. None more so around here than you, dear lady."

"Your assurance is deeply flattering, sir. If you're gonna be odd, do it with flair. That's my motto." She elicited a chuckle from him.

And she was high fashion. The tailored jacket, worn over the corset and chemise, sported wide cuffed sleeves and buttoned up the front with white bands bordering each side of the bodice. Short skirting added elegance at her waistline. A white collar embellished her throat and white cuffs fastened at her wrists beneath the cuffs.

The skirt wasn't cut as full as her formal gown, though it was longer. She'd ditched her petticoats and wore sleek leather pants beneath the skirt, and black riding boots.

"That hat is really something." He traced his finger over the iridescent green feather on one side of the turned-up brim. Black velvet bows decorated the other side. Made of black felt, her slouched hat formed a point at her forehead.

He dropped his gaze to meet her eyes. "You are too fancy to do more than pose, sweetheart, might mess yourself up."

"Don't even go there," she flung back. "This outfit may have been intended for picture taking, but I can ride in it."

"Useful, as that's our aim. However, I have inquired and the Wengers do not have a ladies' side saddle." He gave an apologetic shrug.

"I expected as much." She also suspected he'd known that before asking the family. "I can ride astride. There's a slit in the front of my skirt, concealed by a fold. Grandmother had it added so I can look the part but ride more safely. Side saddles are dangerous."

He lifted a cautioning hand. "That's as may be, but you will scandalize the neighbors."

"I'm already well on my way to shocking, aren't I?"

"You will be viewed as a perfect hoyden riding astride, Evie."

An impatient huff escaped her. "Isn't it strange how people back home—in the future, I mean—think I'm a *perfect lady* in this attire, even riding astride? They're totally wowed by the outfit. Besides, it's like being in a play. No one expects me to get every prop correct."

He squinted at her as if attempting to work out a foreign concept. "You act the part for them?"

"Yes. Otherwise I would be riding in blue jeans." At the arch in his brow, she added, "A sturdy cotton twill fabric called denim is used for jeans—fitted trousers. Trust me, you would look awesome in a pair."

For a jaw-dropping moment, he simply stared at her. "You wear trousers?"

"Some of the time."

Lines deepened on his forehead, and he eyed her incredulously. He bent toward her, his lips parted to speak, vacillated, and then tried again. "The future must be a vastly different place than this realm."

"Yes, but I have a pair of leather pants on now beneath my habit. I think women did that historically, though—"

He stopped her with fingers pressed to her lips. "Again, you speak of history. Live *now*, Evie."

"Breakfast, Jack!" a woman called from below.

"Coming!" Dropping his hand from her mouth, he extended his arm with a gentlemanly flourish. "Shall we proceed?"

She planted a hand on her hip. "Have we agreed I

am riding astride?"

He smiled ruefully. "I think I cannot dissuade you."

"You've got that right." She linked her arm with his. "A pity we aren't riding to hounds with me dressed for it."

"Do you go fox hunting in your other life?"

"Heavens no. I was only joking." She lifted her head. "But I bet I could leap walls and fences on my mare."

"Or break your neck in the effort."

"Or that," she allowed.

Feeling regal with her arm in his, she lifted a length of the skirts with her free hand, so she didn't stumble as they descended the steps. She was glad he wasn't escorting her to the privy. He'd done that earlier this morning with her wrapped in a blanket.

He bent his head near her ear. "The family might wonder why you were not attired in this costume last evening, as presumably we journeyed here on horseback."

"Dang it. You're right. There's a lot about me that doesn't hold up upon closer inspection."

"And much that does." He squeezed her arm and strode with her across the parlor.

Appetizing scents hastened them to the kitchen. Kindling crackled in the cast iron stove crouched in the cozy room like a companionable beast. The vital range gave off warmth while cooking food and heating water and made the kitchen the heart of the house. Evie liked this room best, and always had.

The family was gathered in expectation of having breakfast guests. Their hostess, Mary, gaped at the new bride, likely staggered by her attire. With what must have been near herculean effort, the normally outspoken female bit back any comments.

"Sit, sit." She gestured for the pair to slide onto the bench spanning the expansive table.

Goggling girls clustered on either side of the couple. The remainder of the seven sisters spread over the bench across from them, while their parents sat in the high-backed chairs at either end of the table. Stools for extra family or guests stood nearby. It was a squash fitting everyone around the board, but they had room enough.

Friendlier this way, Evie thought, enjoying the camaraderie and easy laughter that followed the reverent blessing of the food.

Although the sisters resembled each other in appearance, they had distinct personalities, and she would enjoy getting to know each of them better if the girls could get past her outlandish clothes and hair. Outlandish to them, anyway. She would fit in with the upper classes of Victorian society, not that she preferred that strata; she liked these down-to-earth people, their kindness, and gentle nature.

Despite the ongoing challenges of war, spirits were high around the Mennonites' humble table. She hated to dampen their good humor. At the same time, a sense of urgency rose in her

Would Jack wait until later to be the bearer of bad news? It might be best if he told them before he and she rode out, even though she cringed at the thought of spoiling this happy breakfast. He'd agreed the family must be warned if what she'd told him was, indeed, coming.

'It is," she'd affirmed, wishing she had anything hopeful to add. 'Beginning September twenty-sixth.'

Now, it was up to him. After learning today was September twenty-third, several days later than he'd realized, having lost track of time, her message grew more critical. But he seemed reluctant to break into the happy chatter, and lingered over his breakfast, savoring each swallow.

To everyone's delight, the aroma of coffee mingled with the mouthwatering scents of fried bacon and newly baked cornbread thickly spread with apple butter. Scrambled eggs were heaped in yellow mounds in the blue stoneware bowl made by a local potter. This piece had been saved from the fire and now belonged to her grandmother. How strange to see the bowl here in its original setting.

Everything served was fresh and homemade. Paul sipped his coffee from an earthen-colored pottery mug. No milk for him; he drank his black.

Sighing with satisfaction, he nodded at the couple. "What a blessing you have brought to this house. We never thought to see *kaffi* again for months, mayhap years. Your grandmother gave you a wonderful gift, Mrs. Ramsey. You will tell her of our gratitude at sharing in this bounty?"

Evie blotted her lips on a linen square. "Yes. I will."

"About that…" Jack nudged her, giving her a meaningful glance when she looked his way. "Evie and I would like you to keep the coffee in appreciation of your hospitality to us."

Swallowing a gulp, she did her best not to appear as floored as she felt, or the family would think her reluctant. How he could part with the coffee, she couldn't fathom. They still had the instant kind, but he'd been over the moon at finding the bag of roasted beans. His generosity and their awestruck expressions nearly moved her to tears.

If he were willing to relinquish something this special to him, then she mustn't begrudge them the gift. Perhaps they would see her heart was in the right place, even if her choice of dress was unfathomable to them. She'd fall into the category of peculiar people who, nonetheless, 'would do anything for you,' another Gladys McIntyre saying.

"Please take it. Do." She raised her voice to be heard over the spirited protest circling the assembly. "We want you to have it, only be sure you hide the bag well."

Even though Jack hadn't yet cautioned the family about the coming hellfire, he had said Rebels sometimes raided Mennonite farms, as they were easy prey and resented for their pacifism and Union sympathies. These people would have to be wary of threats from both sides of this wretched war, soon to escalate beyond their worst imaginings. Maybe the secreted coffee would offer some small comfort in the dark days ahead.

Paul nodded his grizzled head. "*Denki.* We will hide this rare gift with much care."

A wave of sentiment engulfed Evie to think a product she could purchase in any modern grocery store was so prized.

Mary smiled through winking tears. "You are a good man, Jack Ramsey, you and your new wife, Evie, to share with us."

"You have always shared with me. We are good friends, *ya*?" he prompted.

"Y*a*." The emotion in her brown eyes softened their sharpness.

"You have been like family to me, when my own father rejected me." Huskiness edged his voice.

Capped heads nodded in solemn acknowledgement.

"And now." He cleared his throat, the challenge of what he had to say heavy in his eyes. "I must caution you about a heinous event soon to come our way."

The gathering stiffened, and each head swiveled toward him. "What is this dreadful thing you speak of?" Paul voiced what must be on everyone's mind.

Evie waited, gripping the edge of the table with her fingers. Did Jack believe her enough to stick his neck all the way out and tell them everything? How would they take it?

Looking like he'd rather be anywhere than here imparting this painful news, he circled his gaze at the table. "I must check the accuracy of my information to be sure, but it seems Union Major General Sheridan is heading our way with a large army."

Confusion filled Mary's eyes. "But this is good, *ya*? This Union general will take our part. Have we not been loyal to the Union, and labored to live among Confederate neighbors who hate us for our beliefs?"

Jack was grim. "Yes, you have been faithful and suffered much, but no, Sheridan will not reward you. My contact tells me he will burn your farms and mills to the ground, take your food, steal your animals, or shoot them. All. Every single one."

The horror in their faces seared Evie's soul. But it

was the God's honest truth.

Stoic Paul had the look of one peering into the bowels of Hell while trying not to appear overly upset by the view. "The ways of worldly men are unknown to me. Why would this general visit such suffering on the innocent?"

"I wager he has orders to render our green valley a wasteland, so it can no longer support Rebel troops," Jack said flatly. "We are known as the breadbasket of the Confederacy."

Mary clenched work-worn hands. "But it is not only the Rebels who will go hungry. Women and children, wee babes, old men, the sick and wounded, will suffer want. And all those poor animals killed? This is too terrible."

The images crowding Evie's mind appalled her. If only they could derail the freight train roaring at them that was history. But how? She and Jack couldn't oppose an army.

He nodded gravely at Mary's lament. "If Sheridan does what I'm told he intends, it will be beyond enduring except for the stoutest souls. Many will be forced to flee their homes. This is why you must conceal grain and hay where it cannot be stolen or burned. Seclude your animals in the woods or set them free among the trees to seek for later. All valuables must be hidden."

He turned to Paul. "What of the secret place dug in the rock wall of the cellar? How much will it hold?"

The older man looked at him hard. "Crocks of apple butter, several hams, a sack of cornmeal, household goods, the coffee… This hidey hole is like a small larder."

"Well, fill it up. Expand if you can," Jack directed. "But don't hide anything in the house. It may be burned."

Gasps of horror followed this, but no words. Silence weighted with unspeakable sorrow enfolded the stunned family.

He exhaled heavily. "My best advice is to preserve whatever you can over these next few days. Little time remains. Hide grain in the woods. Find some means to keep it from the damp. Have you barrels?"

Paul gave a nod. "Some. And we have flour and cornmeal in sacks."

"Good. That's something." A shade of relief tinged Jack's somber gaze. "Conceal them in the woods. Keep only a small hidden stock on hand. Pile your hay among the trees, too. Cover everything with branches. Use whatever you can find to form a brushy barrier. The soldiers will be wary of woods."

His creviced brow deeply furrowed, Paul asked, "Why?"

Jack stared into the distance as if at a place he knew and despised. "When Sheridan's army comes it won't be in a solid block of men, but soldiers spread out for miles. They will divide into parties to carry out their destruction," he predicted. "Rebels will stalk the invaders from familiar woods and back roads, making the invaders wary of thickets—anywhere bushwhackers might hide."

Mary twisted her apron round and round. "I cannot believe this. The war on our very doorsteps. Will there be fighting and shooting nearby?"

"Possibly. Keep the girls near the house when the soldiers draw close. I will ride out this morning and see what more I can learn." Jack's eyes were pools of pity. "I am taking Evie with me. May we borrow your gray mare?"

"*Ya*." Paul spoke as if dazed.

The girls appeared too shocked to speak. They sat with tears in their eyes and trickling down pale, freckled cheeks. Evie looked from one stricken face to the other. She had no idea what to say. This might be the right moment to bring out the chocolate bars.

Like a fluffed-up hen, Mary roused to life. "You take care out there, Jack Ramsey. If you are caught, you know what may follow."

He nodded, grim awareness in his eyes, and she beckoned to her daughters. "Come, girls. We have much work to do. Keep a prayer on your lips and courage in your hearts."

Admiration swelled in Evie. The woman had just been told her farm and possibly her home would be burned, all her animals taken or destroyed, unless well hidden, along with her family's food and harvested crops. And yet, like a captain marshalling her troops, she was preparing for battle.

Could Evie do less?

Chapter Nine

While Evie waited for him in the yard, Jack entered the top floor of the two-level red barn built into the side of a gently sloping bank. Called a bank barn, the upper level served as the threshing floor and storage area. Cows milled below, snatching mouthfuls of the hay tossed down to them through the square opening in the floor. Their breathy snorts carried up to him.

He inhaled the sweet aroma from the great golden mound heaped in the mow and on one side of the floor. The hay scent mingled with the familiar bovine aroma central to the farm. Yellow ears of dried corn filled a crib and brown wheat kernels were piled in the bin, adding their graininess to the fragrant blend.

The center of the barn floor provided a generous work area and the door was wide enough to drive a wagon through to load and unload. This feature was important. The Wengers would need to haul food for man and beast to the woods for safekeeping.

Whatever the family couldn't conceal behind the rock wall of their cellar must be hidden elsewhere or lost. Their large draft horse, Bill, would be vital for pulling these loads. Bill was secluded among the trees with their mare, Polly, her foal, and Jack's faithful mount, Buck. The other horses belonging to the Wengers had been confiscated by Rebels, along with some of their livestock.

Half a dozen remaining cows, several calves, a handful of pigs, and their small flock of sheep must also be relocated. Preserving these animals was crucial to the family's survival. There was much work to be done and not a lot of time to do it. The sooner he and Evie rode off and gained information about Sheridan's movements, and returned to be of help to the Wengers, the better.

He lifted his gaze to the rafters of the arched ceiling lined with hand-hewn beams. Dust motes floated in the light streaming through the window set in the uppermost T-shaped front of the barn. Crisscrossed lattice-work covered the airy opening and edged the top of the walls beneath the roof to allow ventilation. The strong breeze blowing this morning easily found its way through the small openings between the strips. Weighty beams and trusses, joined by wooden pegs, held the big timbered structure together.

A pang knifed through him at the thought of all this reduced to a burned-out ruin. *What a waste.*

Normally, the barn was a comforting place, a sanctuary offering reassurance of provision made for the coming winter. *No longer.*

War was detestable; the destruction wreaked on innocent civilians the worst. It sickened him to think of the Wengers and countless other families like them forced to endure the horrific suffering Evie had predicted. And he was determined to do all in his power to aid his friends.

Clenching gloved hands, he strode over scattered hay to the far wall. The floor creaked beneath his boots, and more dust rose. A bridle hung from a peg alongside Bill's harness. The remaining saddle, not yet carried off, was tucked in a dark corner. He needed the equipment for the mare Evie was to ride.

Groaning at the thought of the astonishing effect she'd have on everyone they encountered—not only in her far-flung attire but by riding astride—he took the bridle from the wall. *So be it.*

He hoisted the saddle in his arms, grabbed the horse blanket, and strode outside. *Whew.* He whistled softly.

She glowed with as much appeal as the sunny fall day. *More.* It was all he could do not to drop everything to whirl her in his arms and kiss her, but they were undertaking a serious, quite possibly dangerous, mission.

He needed more information to judge how best to act. Although, he had to admit, what she'd told him was astounding. Unless she truly came from the future, as she'd maintained, he could only think she must be a farsighted seer. Odd, how she spoke of the future as if it were the past. He'd pondered this phenomenon without reaching a definite conclusion.

Maybe she was exactly who she said she was, but it made no sense. She couldn't journey back and forth in time, as if climbing up and down a staircase. Could she?

How on earth was he to grasp this being that was Evie? The unique girl would confound the wisest among them.

****

Breathing in the fresh earthiness of the meadow, Evie lifted her gaze to the white clouds scudding overhead. The endlessly arching blue sky met the hills rising across the field like a mini Swiss Alps. Gold light gilded the beads of dew sparkling on each blade of grass and shining leaf like jewels sprinkled by the hands of fairies.

Yellow, red, and saffron hues mingling with the green foliage on the trees proclaimed autumn upon them, rather disorienting as it had been June for her only yesterday. The crisp breeze tugging at her hair made her glad for the wool riding habit and kidskin gloves, but this cooler weather was ideal for a canter across the countryside with Jack.

Because of him, her senses were heightened. Everything struck her with greater intensity than before. Colors were brighter, sounds clearer, and scents richer. For better or worse, she was acutely aware and felt more alive than ever.

She smiled up at him. "What a perfect day for riding."

The wide-brimmed slouch hat shaded his face, and he bore the bridle, saddle, and blanket he'd retrieved from the barn for the mare hidden in the woods. He frowned. "We're on a mission to gather information, not a pleasure outing."

Reality came crashing back. "I know, buzzkill, but we can still have fun."

"*Warily*," he emphasized. "And what the Sam Hill is a buzzkill?"

"Wet blanket, killjoy, Debbie downer... You get the drift."

An expression of wry humor crossed his shadowed eyes. "I grasp your meaning. And don't call me Debbie. Has a girlish sound."

"Deal, and it's only a saying. I'm living *now*, as you urged me," she quoted back at him.

"Good to hear. Just keep your wits about you."

"Done. I'm on it." But being with Jack was electrifying, and distracting, as was the glorious day.

Lifting her skirts above the sea of grass, she followed at his side, thrilled he'd allowed her to accompany him and not left her behind. She was on an adventure with her rugged cowboy. How cool was that?

He shifted the saddle in his arms. "When we are finished riding, I will conceal this horse tack in the trees with mine. Better the damp than risk the stuff being burned or stolen."

Tension tightened her spine. "It's hard to believe such evil is coming with all this beauty around us."

"You have declared it so," he said, striding through the grass. "And in my heart, I fear it to be true."

"Yes." She quickened her pace to keep up with him. "You saw how near the barn is to the house?"

He answered with a somber nod.

In her mind's eye, she compared the Wengers' red barn with the one on Grandma G.'s herb farm. "Depending on the wind, fire could spread between the two structures. The barn built in its place stands farther away."

The bridle jingled as he walked. "Perhaps from a sad lesson learned.

"Perhaps. The proximity of the two buildings might be how the house catches fire, if the soldiers didn't intentionally set the blaze. I recall accounts of men who did that very thing, even going from room to room and kindling a fire to be certain it took. Heartless."

"War brings out the worst in men. Yet there are those who resist the call to darkness." He spoke as if from experience.

"True. Not all soldiers in the accounts I've heard were said to be callous," she admitted. "Some even refused to take part in the Burning, or did the least harm they could, but the sadists in the ranks reveled in their cruelty."

Jack wore the look of one who had witnessed the darkest souls in action. "This can be said of both sides in this bloody conflict."

"I can well imagine." They walked on in silence, the country sounds resonating around them.

Elusive meadowlarks trilled from the grass bending in the wind. Somewhere a hound bayed. A horse whinnied. Chickens clucked and squabbled from the barnyard they'd left behind them. Quacking ducks flew past with that peculiar wobble in their flight, and a long V of geese honked overhead.

An idyllic scene, if only the war would leave this lush valley alone.

Baa! A wooly ewe scuttled aside at their approach and startled Evie. She lost her footing on the slick grass and lurched forward, stumbling on her hem.

"Careful." Jack snaked out his hand to grab her arm, and kept her from smacking on the wet ground.

"Thanks," she gasped, regaining her balance. "These darn skirts will be the death of me."

"Stay alert. We scarcely know what day it is, let alone when the Boys in Blue are coming."

"True." She only had a vague recollection of dates. "The war seems leagues away on this pristine morning."

"It's not."

"No." The warning inside told her otherwise, like a

tolling bell.

They crossed the meadow, the ground sloping as they neared the hills. They began the ascent. His long strides covered ground faster than her shorter legs, and she swept her skirts away from rocks in the limestone outcropping.

As they proceeded, he angled glances over his shoulder and side-to-side, while eyeing the woods ahead. Did he expect someone to show himself? Sam Hobbs, from last night, perhaps?

Jack slowed and let her catch her breath. "Be vigilant. Remember, Rebel guerillas could appear from anywhere, in either direction."

"A grave reminder, and difficult for me to grasp." She found herself falling into old-fashioned phrasing, perhaps from the past life she didn't really remember. "These woods appear much as they do in the future. I have picked violets here in the spring and teaberries in autumn and they have always been quite safe."

"It's not the trees that do the attacking, Evie."

"No. Despite the danger, or perhaps because of it, this lovely place seems dearer to me, and I feel responsible for it. In a way, this is my home. Yours, too."

His pensive air indicated he was considering her claim. "I have a cabin in the mountains."

"You had this home first, way back when. We both did," she reasoned.

He slowly inclined his head, a depth of emotion behind his silent concession.

Satisfied with his acknowledgement, she turned toward the patchwork of fields below them. The golden-brown stubble from harvested crops spread alongside green meadows. In the distance, fields outlined by rail fences contained sheep, cows, and horses. Much of the harvested grain had been stored in barns. Here and there, sheaves of wheat stood bundled together with their heads upright. She also spotted corn shocks.

What artistic arrangements, and so fallish. She didn't see these much in modern-day fields, though Grandma G. had as a girl. Cooing gray doves fluttered between the sheaves in search of spilled seed. Reddish brown and white quail darted among the other foragers. The doves were familiar, but bobwhite had grown scarce in the valley of the future.

Admiration welled in her. "How beautiful."

"Yes. Farmers work hard to tend the land and suffer the most when it's trampled by war. See the *stooks*?" He pointed at the autumnal mounds.

"You mean the shocks?"

"Same thing," he said. "*Stooks* is a German expression. They are left to dry for later use."

"Only later won't come for these unfortunate folks, and harvest has been good, by the looks of it. How unfair, Jack."

He gave a solemn nod. "Aye. Crops are among the very best, which means winter will be extra hard this year. Nature compensates."

"But man doesn't." She recoiled at the thought of the misery to come. "The fruits of their labor will be torn from these people, and there aren't enough places to hide such abundance."

"Only a fraction of the crops can be saved, even with warning. Let us learn all we can about Sheridan's actions, then we will better be able to plan." He spoke in the calm manner of a man accustomed to reasoning.

Regret needled her. "You need specifics, and I only remember fragments."

He paused. "Perhaps more will occur to you."

"More than I thought possible already has." She puzzled over the gaps in her memory. "Can I expect greater recall, do you suppose?"

"We shall see." With the ghost of a smile, he gestured ahead at the thick woods. "The horses are hidden there. When danger nears, we hide them in a sinkhole among the trees."

"How do you get the horses in it without breaking their legs?"

He gave her a look. "It's not *that* deep, more of a large bowl in the earth that they can be led in and out of. When they are in the sinkhole they know to be quiet."

"Really?" She was impressed. "That's perceptive of them."

"Horses have more sense than many people." Disdain edged his observation.

"I agree." She studied the tossing branches for any suspicious movement, detected only squirrels scurrying up a scarlet oak, and returned her attention to the vista spreading beyond them.

While the land was idyllically pastoral in the future, it was simpler now, like *The Shire* in *The Lord of the Rings*. These country folk, especially the Mennonites and other plain people, reminded her a little of the Hobbits. They were equally unprepared for what was bearing down on them.

A dirt road ran past the farm, the grassy verge starred with goldenrod, late Queen Anne's lace, and fluffy white milkweed pods bending in the wind. When taken in a westerly direction, the earthen track led to the Alleghenies. If followed the opposite way, the road ran to the town of Harrisonburg, the seat of Rockingham County, and their destination.

God only knew who they'd meet on their ride, but Jack said Harrisonburg was the place to discover what was afoot. Unless they encountered someone en route who could provide the answers, he'd added.

If only they were going for a joy ride instead of facing possible life and death situations. Being a former Confederate officer, now Unionist guide scouting for information, Jack was at greater risk than she. Either side could take him for a member of the other. She hoped by being with him, she could help defray violence, while realizing it was a stretch.

She surveyed the route they must take. "I cannot say for certain when rough men clad in blue will appear to destroy this Eden."

He waved at the road. "Not yet. We can see for miles from this vantage point. I only detect a farmer hauling hay in a wagon, and girls herding sheep across the road."

Her gaze traveled more distantly than ever in this unpolluted terrain. "Yes. The land is much the same as this in the future, except my grandmother's herb farm is tucked in among the other holdings."

"What else is changed?" He seemed genuinely curious.

"We have tall wooden poles with wires strung between them to carry electricity, and telephone lines, for one thing."

"Unknown to me."

"Not for long. Enormous inventions are coming to America after the war," she said. "But I like this uncluttered landscape. We also have farm machinery, cars, trucks, wire fences, lofty silos, signs, and other modern additions."

A frown tightened his mouth. "What if you do not want these things?"

"There is only so much we can do without, unless we live way back in the mountains. Then you can escape."

Relief tinged his gaze. "Good. There is a way out."

"Yes, and some Mennonites and Amish still live much as they are now." She studied him earnestly. "I really think you would like a pickup truck, though."

He met her gaze with bemusement on his face. "I have no knowledge of what you speak."

"I pray you will."

Gravity darkened his eyes a deeper shade of greenish-brown. "If I wish to remain here, will you stay with me?"

A sinking sensation weighed her chest. She loathed telling him the truth, and hesitated, then plunged ahead like a bolting horse. "You can't stay here much longer, Jack, even if I agreed."

His scrutiny intensified. "Why is that?"

"You don't survive this war. Grandma G. told me. And there are some things history refuses to alter."

"Huh." A breathy exhalation escaped him, and his shoulders sagged. "Not one for holding back, are you?"

"No." Hating herself, she pressed on. "So, when it's time for us to go to the future, please come with me. I will get us through."

A dubious glint flickered in his eyes. "How can

you be certain?"

"I'm not. But Grandma G. is, and she has a way of being right. And, in her, we must trust."

His forehead creased beneath his hat, and he pursed his lips. "What of God? I'm not a complete heathen."

"Nor I, and I expect God sent me. It's all kind of mixed up."

"It certainly is," he said in clipped accents. "Come on. Let's saddle those horses. We will be all day if we stand about talking." Straightening his shoulders, he strode ahead.

"But Jack—" Evie broke off. This wasn't the time. Abandoning her plea, she hastened after him.

Chapter Ten

In the woods above the Wenger farm, small whirlwinds Evie called dust devils spun the first fallen leaves. The rich scent of crumbling earth and living plants rode on the strong breeze. Glances between the furrowed trunks revealed scenery much the same as she recalled from recent memory. It was reassuring to see the woods were largely unchanged.

Drifts of fern traced with tawny hues grew among the velvety moss. Creeping wintergreen plants dotted with the red berries she enjoyed picking trailed over the leafy ground. Purple asters and yellow daisy-like flowers flourished where the sunlight slanted through the leafy canopy. Mitten-shaped sassafras leaves fluttered alongside silvery barked sycamores and sweet gums with their spiky balls. Maples changing into vivid autumn colors kept company with red and bronze oaks. Tossing evergreens were interspersed throughout.

Tiny chipmunks scurried over a lichen encrusted log and squirrels ran up and down the trees gathering nuts for winter storage. Late butterflies fluttered above dappled blossoms, some of the ephemeral creatures more brightly colored than the flowers they visited. Everywhere, birds created a symphony of sound.

Such a serene spot. A secluded picnic with Jack would be heaven, but they couldn't stop now. Thirsty from the uphill walk, beating at skirts whipping in the wind, she'd sipped from his tin, drum-shaped canteen. The metallic flavored water in the Confederate container reminded her a little of her late grandfather's Marine Corps canteen. She well recalled its tepid metallic taste.

A last glance around the comforting woods and she prodded herself into action. While Jack held the mare's head, stroking her muzzle and soothing her with quiet words, she fit her boot into the stirrup and swung herself into the saddle. Polly hadn't ever been ridden by a woman in a riding habit before, and never by Evie. The mare was also reluctant to leave her six-month-old chestnut colt. The leggy boy was tethered near the big reddish-brown draft horse, Bill, who had the temperament of a teddy bear. Bill helped steady the foal, and the mare would soon settle down. If all went as planned, the three horses would be reunited by late afternoon.

If… The uncertain word circled in Evie's mind like the swirling leaves.

She adjusted her skirts on either side of the mare, making sure the fabric fell evenly without a display of her legs. The breeze didn't assist her efforts at modesty. Even though she wore leather pants under her habit, she didn't want to shock the locals any more than she already was. After the Wengers' jaw-dropping reaction to her attire at breakfast, she no longer questioned her likely effect on the wider community.

Crop in hand, she firmed her grip on the reins. "I'm as ready as I'm going to be, Jack."

A brief but glorious smile lit his face. "A rare vision , like an exotic butterfly."

His praise was a warm washing wave, but she

wanted to be taken seriously. "Not too exotic to sit the saddle, Jack."

"Yes. Yes."

The hint of condescension in his tone irked her.

He untethered his patient mount, Buck, the same shade as his buff leather gloves, with a black mane and tail. The horse was striking, as was its master. "Keep close watch as we go along, and *heed me*," he said pointedly, as if she wouldn't otherwise.

Annoyance flashed in her like heat lightning. "I'm not devoid of judgement."

"Never said you were," he tossed over his shoulder.

"Near enough. You have to realize, women are more independent and outspoken where I come from."

He countered with an eye roll. "Strong minded females have plenty to say here, as well. The reverse of your assertion is also true. You don't know this place. Follow. Don't lead."

"I wasn't planning to," she shot back. "Merely point out things you may have missed and offer advice when needed."

Giving a snort, he said, "How do you think that might sound to a commanding officer?"

"Overreaching. But you aren't my commander."

"Good thing, too. You don't understand *follow*." He swung onto Buck, looking spectacular seated in the saddle.

Her admiring gaze never left his handsome figure. "There are times when assertiveness is called for."

"I trust you will ferret out those occasions." With a devilish grin, he wheeled the horse around. "Try to keep pace," he challenged, and bounded away.

Nobody outdistanced her! Giving Polly a nudge, she sprang after him on the obliging mare. The two horses cleared the woods and pounded down the hill, Jack out in front on Buck.

Sod flew beneath their hooves as they galloped across the meadow. The wind chilled Evie's face, tugging at her hair and clothes. If her hat hadn't been secured with a length of gauze, it would have flown off.

Bent low in the saddle, the scent of grassy earth in her nose, she urged Polly on. The mare would tire sooner than the hardened gelding, and lag behind him. For now, her long gray legs devoured the field. She closed in on Buck's tail.

Jack galloped his swift mount at the split rail fence bordering the meadow. The horse sailed over the wooden barrier with blue sky showing between his hooves and the top rails. Buck landed securely on the springy turf, and Jack reined in. Evie launched the mare over the divide and planted her beside him. She drew up, glowing with pride.

"Bravo." Jack tipped his hand to her. "You ride as well as you claimed."

"Thank you, sir." She reveled in proving herself, and the spark of indignation faded. "I admit you may have a point. I can be a bit impulsive."

A smile warmed his eyes. "Indeed."

She patted the mare's glossy neck. "There's a saying about discretion being the better part of valor. I'll bear it in mind."

"A wise adage.

"But that's all. I'm not changing drastically for you." Especially not if she got stuck in this era.

"I would not want you to." He dropped his voice.

111

"Observe extreme caution from here on out. No shenanigans."

She wasn't sure what a shenanigan was, let alone how to get up to one. "What?"

"Check your high spirits."

She nodded, and he motioned her forward. "Onward."

Kicking up dust, they cantered down the lane and onto the road. Jack slowed Buck, motioning her beside him on his left. She eased Polly between the gelding and the grassy verge. He kept to the outer edge. They maintained a brisk trot, Evie still glowing from the bracing ride.

Not Jack. Her silent companion constantly swept his gaze at the fields on every side. Taking the hint from him, she said nothing. He tensed when they passed copses of trees and narrow lanes forking off.

His apprehension was contagious. What he'd said about Rebels hiding in thickets and back roads returned to her, and she scrutinized every shadow. If men were gunning for him, they'd made themselves invisible. She hoped her presence would discourage an attack, but there was no guarantee.

To those who didn't know any differently, Jack resembled a Confederate rider. The Rebel scouts were aware of his desertion, though, and oncoming Union soldiers wouldn't differentiate. She wished she were better equipped to be of help if trouble arose. All she could do was pray they got there and back okay.

The journey wore on. She noted the farms they wound past were situated farther apart than their modern equivalents. None of the small subdivisions lining the road or nestled among the hills existed in this day. She recognized few of the brick and white frame houses that did stand. It nagged her that she should know more of these homes, if they'd survived. Unless the structures had fallen into disrepair and been replaced, only one obvious explanation accounted for their disappearance. They must have been burned down.

A grim thought.

Now and then, they rode by farmers who paused in their labors, hay fork half way to the wagon, or crossing the barnyard toting buckets, and gaped at her. Women and children stopped digging potatoes or gathering eggs and stood, mouths ajar. One wide-eyed little girl hugged a pet duck. Their astonishment would be comical if the winds of war weren't sweeping this way.

Jack nodded at them, and Evie waved. She would be the talk of the neighborhood. Sadly, these people would soon have far more pressing matters on their minds than her outlandish appearance. An unknown lady in high fashion riding astride would take a distant back seat to what was coming.

The pungent aroma of animals reminded her of their endangerment. She liked the hominess of livestock and didn't mind the odors. It grieved her to think of the cows, pigs, sheep, and horses, even poultry, that would soon be herded away, or shot.

How empty the land would be without them. She prayed many animals were taken to safety before it was too late. But would they be? Should she and Jack shout warning as they passed?

He didn't seem inclined even to speak to her, let alone these others. Perhaps they might call out on their return?

Still, no one emerged to threaten them, and they hadn't yet seen any other riders. Strange to be on a road empty of the soldiers destined to charge their way, and even more peculiar to travel without the cars and trucks that normally sped over this stretch of highway, now dirt track. She didn't miss the vehicles or the cyclist with a death wish who tore past Lavender and Lace Herb Farm daily. The absence of traffic made the pocked ground, grooved from wagon wheels, far preferable to the paved but busy road of her experience. Much was gained from progress, and an inestimable amount lost.

Safety first, was her father's motto, and one she embraced. Odd maxim, considering they rode toward war.

It occurred to her that she'd always wondered how communities recovered from catastrophe, without realizing she lived in one with people who had done just that. The Burning had devastated much of the Shenandoah Valley, but resilient residents hung on and fought their way back. No modern-day visitor would guess that horrific event had ever taken place. But it left marks on the landscape, mostly in the missing structures, and stories passed down through families.

Sheridan was still hated and his wing man, George Armstrong Custer, wasn't too popular either. It was generally agreed among older residents that Custer got what was coming to him when he turned his warring ways out west and double-dog dared the Lakota Sioux. Sooty, beleaguered country folk, their property in flames, must have been unspeakably grateful when the Yankee horde finally cleared out, with hundreds of pitiful refugees in tow.

Her future valley might be built up and cluttered in places, but the scenery remained among the most beautiful in the world. This was largely due to the hardworking farmers, especially the Mennonites, who had preserved the land. And, as her grandmother said, 'The land is everything, Evie.'

Those words fully sank in. *Lesson learned, Grandma G.* She hoped to convey her newfound wisdom in person.

They left more farms behind, riding at least four or five miles with Jack on red alert. She was equally wary. It was difficult to tell how near they were to town.

"Closer now," he said, as if gauging her thoughts. He turned toward her. "Are you holding up all right?"

Forcing a smile, she nodded. Scant sleep combined with more excitement in twenty-four hours than most people experienced in a lifetime was taking a toll.

He didn't appear entirely convinced of her satisfactory state, but the thumbs up signal she offered him received a blank look. Wasn't that the universal signal for okay?

Not in this era, apparently. He shook his head and returned his focus to their surroundings. She did the same. None of the familiar landmarks were present to lend her guidance, and she didn't want to ask him how much farther they had to go every five minutes, or he really would think she was ready to drop.

Seriously, Evie? she chided herself. This was her stretch of the valley. She ought to have a clue where they were, but the houses were farther apart than normal.

The added outbuildings, animals, and sprawling vegetable gardens around these homes made them resemble farmettes. The most livestock a modern city dweller could argue for was a handful of hens. No roosters. Maybe they could keep a rabbit.

These large lots must have been chopped into smaller plots in later years. Now, not even the bends and curves in the road were as she recalled, having been altered over time. She only knew the ground was hilly and people were growing thicker than they had been in the heart of the country.

Fortunately, no one troubled them as they trotted up and down hills. Jack stopped to allow the horses a drink from the gurgling stream, while he and she took another metallic swig from his canteen and shared a granola bar. They resumed their trek and entered what must be Harrisonburg.

"We're here," he affirmed, gesturing ahead. "There's the courthouse."

"Yes." She spotted the steeple on the two-story brick structure, more impressive than the other buildings.

When they entered the center of town, he asked, "Recognize anything?"

She strained to see beyond the immediate structures and turned her head from side-to-side. "Some. Not a lot." One stately three-story building stretched on the corner of Court Square resembled a grand hotel, but it was foreign to her. A shame such a fine old place was gone.

The bare bones of what she'd known lay around her, a blink compared to the present-day city Harrisonburg had mushroomed into. Only a few of the larger houses still standing in the twenty-first century, and converted to businesses and museums, were here now. Most of these were built of stone or brick, more enduring materials, though some wood frame structures had also survived. The bulk of the historic homes and buildings she'd admired must date to a later, more affluent era, than this one.

Main Street, she assumed it was, had a row of shops along it, a millinery, and butcher shop among them. A liquor store and tavern were doing brisk trade for wartimes. The tavern would be ideal for gaining information, but she doubted Jack would allow her to enter such a dominantly male establishment.

Should she wait on her mare while he went in? She was hesitant to dismount in case they needed to make a hasty getaway, though she longed for a quiet table in a dark corner. She wanted to sit there with him and have something to eat. She'd settle for a decent drink and a nap.

Horses and riders jogged by them. Wagons jolted past, and a carriage skirted them on the dusty street. The whole scene was like a movie set. Surreal. She had no idea where people were going, but some seemed in a tearing hurry.

"There." Jack grabbed her arm.

He slowed Buck to a walk and she did the same with Polly. "What do you see?" she whispered.

"Confederates."

She looked past the riders and wagons to where he indicated. Ahead of them, were three ragtag men on foot, their pace more of a limp than a walk. They leaned on each other for support as they labored along in uniforms that were more rags than cloth. Haversacks were slung over thin shoulders and they bore muskets and side arms, but their crushed demeanor indicated no use for the weapons. They had no fight left in them. Bloody bandages swathed several limbs and one man's head beneath his gray slouch hat.

Pity swelled in Evie. "Poor boys."

"Yeah," Jack grunted. "They came down the Valley Pike."

"Meaning?" she pressed.

"From the northern end of the valley, where Jubal Early would be battling."

"The Confederate general?" She double-checked.

"Afraid so."

She tried to wrap her weary brain around his insight while a middle-aged woman in brown skirts and a matching bonnet hurried over to the wounded men. She withdrew chunks of bread from a wicker basket and pressed the food into their grimy outstretched hands. "What happened, boys?"

"Sheridan," they croaked in unison.

"We got beat bad. Twice," the bloodiest of the three added hoarsely. None of them looked any older than their early twenties.

The horrified female clapped fingers to her open mouth. "Dear God in heaven."

Jack inhaled sharply. "I reckon Jubal Early got whipped."

"Hasten home and hide all you can, ma'am," one of the three advised between mouthfuls. "We can't do no more for you. We're heading to the hospital."

"Where's the Army of the Valley?" the woman pressed, as a small gathering collected around them.

"Hightailing south, what's left of it."

Dismay engulfed the bystanders. "As bad as that?" asked an older whiskered gentleman in a gray frockcoat and bowler.

"Every bit, and worse," the beaten spokesman assured him. "Get ready, you hear? Sheridan's coming. Ain't no one can stop him now."

The well-dressed man bent toward them. "How many soldiers are with him?"

"Thousands. Like crows covering the sky, blotting out the sun. Be here afore sunset tomorrow."

Evie sagged in the saddle. It had begun.

Jack didn't wait to hear anymore. "Let's go."

Chapter Eleven

What in blazes was Jack to do? Seething with fury and frustration, he wheeled Buck around. The anxious assembly circling the wounded soldiers parted to allow him and Evie through. There was nothing here for these people but despair. Their county seat was about to be overrun. Sheridan would likely make his headquarters in Harrisonburg, blast him.

Jack hadn't expected to be engulfed by anger at the trio's confirmation of Evie's warning, but he was. She somberly followed him on the mare as they navigated streets filling with loaded wagons and hurried civilians. Some folk were getting away while they still could. If they had a carriage and horses, all the better. Those who remained in town would barricade themselves in their homes, and secret food and possessions. Good luck to them, poor wretches.

Damn it all. He had to exert the utmost control not to swear the vilest oaths he could concoct. Not fit for a lady's ears.

Gnashing his teeth would do nothing to remedy the abominable situation, and only cause Evie further distress. But oh, how it goaded him to hear of Sheridan's imminent arrival from the mouths of those who had battled to keep the monster out. How many men had fallen in the attempt he shuddered to think. Guilt stung him for not having fought by their side, while part of him regretted ever having served in the Confederacy in the first place.

He defined *torn.* This only increased his vexation.

They left the dismayed townsfolk behind and Evie drew her mare alongside him and Buck. Together, they trotted the horses up and down the hilly road back the way they had come. The creak of saddles and tread of hooves accompanied their strained journey.

Should he take up arms? His valley was coming under furious attack, and defenders were few. The agonizing quandary raked his troubled mind with each rise and fall of his mount. He had choices, none of them good.

She slid anxious glances at him, as if trying to gauge his mood: black as a moonless sky with no stars. He didn't trust himself to speak and kept his mouth clamped shut.

Finally, she turned toward him, the green feather on her black hat ruffling in the wind, her face drawn with worry. "I can't bear to think of the soldiers burning our home."

Pain ricocheted through him. "It's not ours," he reminded her and himself, annoyed that she had him thinking of the farm in such intimate terms.

The corners of her mouth turned down. "You know what I mean."

He did. *Acutely.* "I have a cabin, out of the reach of the coming flames. The sensible thing would be to go there."

Shock widened her blue-gray eyes, smudged with fatigue. "We can't abandon the Wengers, or the house. It's our portal to the future."

He forced himself to reply with restraint. "I agree

with giving them every support, but you must forgive my difficulty in grasping your assertion. Tell me again what phenomenon you are anticipating?"

"Grandma G. calls it a warble, when the future and past shift back and forth, opening a door between the two. I know it sounds bizarre." Her eyes creased in apology.

"Indeed. Fantastical. Call it what you will, the future you speak of holds no reality for me."

"It will, once you're there." Pleading underlay her insistence.

He strongly doubted he would walk through any peculiar looking ripple if one presented itself and had no intention of letting her go either. Assuming what she spoke of existed. He wasn't convinced. "I cannot contemplate that distant place. The here and now consumes me. I was never more bedeviled."

"No." Strands of hair whipped across her pensive gaze. "Seeing for myself is very different from hearing about it. Jack, I'm scared."

"A tempest brews over our heads. Only a fool would feel no alarm at what's coming."

Sheaves of grain rustled in the wind, and he shifted his brooding focus to the nearby field neatly dotted with *stooks*. Soft scents floated on the stiff breeze. Milkweed fluff, like tiny parasols, sailed to the four corners. Great white clouds patterned the earth in light and shadows, passing over cows grazing in a green pasture, the image of contentment. Sheep baaed, their wooly forms visible on a distant hill. Children ran, laughing, down a lane toward a white frame house, a small dog yipping at their heels. The beauty of this place stabbed him through the heart.

He gestured at their surroundings. "Everything looks as it did when we first rode this way. And yet it's ominously different. Deep down, I had hoped you were mistaken in your dire prophecy."

"So did I, though I didn't see how it could be otherwise," she said, waving kindly at the children. "The wounded soldiers didn't speak of fire, but they gave warning enough. I fear the rest will follow."

Certainty weighed his gut like heavy lead. "An army of the size those three described doesn't come without awful purpose. Sheridan is not on a jaunt, just passing through."

"No." She had the sorrowful demeanor of one poised before a grave. "He's coming to win the war by destroying us."

"Does it work?" Jack flashed back, waving her off before she replied. "Never mind. You told me. We lose."

"Big time." A frown furrowed her smooth brow. "It's as if the valley is punished for the collective sins of the South."

"That hardly seems fair, and with war made against women and children? How brave," he scorned. "Only older men remain here openly, unless they have an exemption. The others are wounded, in hiding, or dead."

She grimaced in agreement.

"This is a most damnable business," he muttered. "Hail with pellets the size of cannon balls could hardly be worse than the retribution you have foretold."

"Not a lot. What will you do?"

The question branded his soul. "What man doesn't fight when war comes to his door belching fire and smoke?"

"Mennonites," she emphasized. "The Wengers and others like them would never take up arms in their defense. Violence of any sort is against their beliefs."

He sighed. "With rare exceptions, this is true. Pacifism is the doctrine of their church, and those who depart from it are shunned. But violence isn't against your beliefs, is it?"

Her cheeks flushed a deeper pink than the chill wind accounted for. "I would meet the burners with a pitchfork, or whatever else I could lay my hands on."

Smiling slightly, he envisioned her planted defiantly between the oncomers and the farm. "Many Southern women would do likewise. But I cannot allow you to take that risk."

"You may have to. Union soldiers mustn't find you on the farm when they come. You will be arrested."

"Or worse." He didn't soften the truth and met her searching gaze. "The old Jack would fight without hesitation."

Her face creased in emphatic refusal. "No. It's a lose-lose situation. How can you oppose an army large enough to blot out the sun?"

"I can't, but I can harass the heck out of the smaller parties they will form to execute their vile purpose."

She shook her head. "Dear God. You mustn't."

"I can ride circles around them," he scoffed.

"There are too many. Are you courting death, Jack?"

"Not in the least. This is my land. My valley. I know every road, lane, and track. They are newcomers and at a disadvantage."

"Even so, you cannot possibly guarantee your

safety.

He shrugged. "No one can."

Flames lit her eyes in a meld of anger and pleading. "Grandma G. is trying to aid us."

"From the future? How?"

"She brought us supplies, and advised me," Evie fired back. "She may do more. I don't know."

"You said your grandmother told you I don't survive this war. Maybe it's my destiny to fall opposing these destroyers?"

Evie appeared angry enough to kill him herself. "Stop that kind of talk right now, mister. I don't think this is how Grandma G. meant. But if you're bent on being foolhardy, you may alter your end. Then how am I to save you?"

"I don't expect you to," he snapped.

Tears welled in her reproachful gaze, and he gentled his tone. "If you are meant to find a way to aid me, you will. But I cannot stand idly by while bluecoats destroy my valley."

"Who said anything about idle? We must spread warning. People in town know an army's coming, but that's the extent of their knowledge, and folk in the country are unaware."

"We will tell a few," he agreed. "But they must help spread word. We haven't the time to ride all over the countryside, and you look ready to keel over." Fresh guilt stung him. "I forget how accustomed I am to days in the saddle, while you are not."

"It isn't only the long ride that has tired me, and I've been on those, but the change in time. Worse than jet lag, or losing an hour from daylight saving, and I know you don't understand a word I just said."

"No need. You admitted your fatigue." And there was some satisfaction in that small victory.

"Well…yes. But how can I rest with all the work that must be done to help the family prepare for the worst?"

"I shall work while you sleep after we return. Then tomorrow—"

A shot exploded, sending a bullet whizzing past his ear.

Confound it! He'd let his attention drift while debating with Evie. The trees on his left partly hid a narrow track leading off into the countryside. An ideal spot for an ambush. How could he have missed it?

"Stay back," he hissed at her, cursing his negligence. He could be dead in an instant. Then what would happen to Evie?

Seizing the revolver at his waist, he swung Buck toward the secluded spot. Eyes intent, he probed every leafy shadow. There! A figure obscured by trees and underbrush waited on horseback. He took aim.

"Hold up, Jack."

At the distinctly familiar and unwelcome voice, he paused, his finger on the trigger. "You weary of following me around, Sam Hobbs?"

"Sure am." The branches parted, and Sam emerged on a big red horse, his pistol also drawn. That had been a warning shot. The sharp-eyed scout rarely missed.

"Who you got with you?" Amazement widening his eyes, Sam reined in his mount and lowered his gun. "You're a sly one, Jack. Who's the lady? Not one of your usual rescues. Kept her a secret, haven't you?"

Relaxing his guard slightly, wondering at Sam's intentions, he grunted in the affirmative. "My wife,

Evie McIntyre, from Augusta County," he replied, giving him a nugget to chew on. "And yes, I have guarded her. Wouldn't you, *Cousin*?" he pressed, aware of her astonishment.

"Uh huh." The opposing man appeared equally taken aback. Walking the horse closer, he nodded at Evie. "Pleased to meet you, ma'am. I know some of your kin. Staunch Confederates. What are you doing with my renegade cousin?"

"Jack? You're the renegade," she sputtered.

"By *his* account, you mean." Sam reined in his mount again and gaped at her.

She shifted her baffled gaze from one to the other. "You two are nearly identical. Did you realize?"

Laughing, Sam thumbed back a wide-brimmed gray hat. "Yeah. Except one of us is crazy."

"You," Jack retorted, but he didn't argue the undeniable family resemblance. "We were like twins growing up."

Sam snorted. "And tussled like a pair of bull calves."

They'd also had each other's backs until this damn war came between them. Sam had the same hazel gaze, chiseled chin beneath the stubble, shoulder length blond hair, and lanky frame, though Jack liked to think he was the better looking, definitely the nobler, of the two. There was no accounting for the marital taste of his father's sister in her choice of spouse. Apart from that, Aunt Ida seemed sane enough. His late uncle must have passed on the inherent wild streak in Sam.

The fellow smelled of wood smoke, pipe tobacco, and pronounced masculinity. His faded butternut coat, vest, and pants were the casual attire of a guerilla scout.

He ran with a loosely formed group of partisan rangers who shifted between the valley and West Virginia, raiding Union supplies, chasing down deserters, and retaliating against unionist sympathizers.

These guerillas acted outside the authority of General Lee, and were little more than bushwhackers. But now, Jack considered his kin speculatively. There might be some use for him and his wolf pack.

Taking a chance, he holstered his gun. "You have far greater quarry to stalk than me, Sam. Sheridan's coming."

The sharp scout followed his movement with the barest flicker in his keen gaze. "I heard something of the sort this morning. You know when?"

"Any hour."

"You don't look too happy about that," Sam observed, holstering his pistol. "Thought you might be clicking your heels in joy with your Unionist sympathies."

"No. I would have to be stark raving mad to rejoice. Sheridan will torch everything and kill or cart off all the rest."

"The valley will be a barren wasteland," Evie supplied.

Sam shifted his scrutiny between them. "That so? What are you gonna do about it, cousin of mine?"

The relentless question tormented him. "Not much we can do. But…"

"No, Jack." Evie's fierce whisper elicited the ghost of a smile from his watchful relation.

"I have the family to think of before taking any action," he amended.

"Oh, I wouldn't worry about your papa," Sam

scoffed. "He's likely royally entertaining the bluecoats as we speak."

"Probably so." Jack envisioned his father falling all over himself acting the gracious host. "He will need all his wiles to prevent them from burning his barn on the way out. I wasn't thinking of him, anyway. Not after he disowned me."

"Ah. You mean your adopted brood?" Contempt tightened Sam's sardonic smile, but he bit back the swearing that would normally follow such an admission.

Some choice words rose on Jack's tongue and remained there in Evie's presence. "Yes. I must also consider my wife," he said instead.

"Certainly." His Rebel kin waved a gloved hand, as if giving his blessing, but a mocking smile flickered at his mouth. "See this fair lady settled as best you can. Leaving her with *the family*?"

Indignation swelled in Jack alongside the anger already brewing. "You must admit the Wengers are hardworking and superb farmers."

"Indisputably." A wicked grin curved Sam's lips. "The boys and I have enjoyed many a good meal at their expense."

Jack arched in the saddle, like a panther ready to spring. "No more. You leave them alone."

"I might oblige, if you confide your plans regarding our coming visitors," Sam bargained.

"Simple. I will shadow them like a hawk, hasten their fiery stops, and make their stay here less than agreeable."

"Oh, Jack." Evie heaved a heavy sigh. "You're putting yourself in the thick of it."

He hated to upset her, but there it was. "Someone has to, sweetheart. We can't just let them linger at each farm."

Approval glinted in his former adversary's greenish-brown gaze. "Want any help hurrying the bluecoats along? More safety in numbers."

Running with wolves wasn't Jack's usual mode of operation. But there was nothing normal about the scorching invasion soon to be underway in his beloved valley. Sheridan had left him no choice, and this meeting with his cousin might prove propitious. "Half a dozen or so men would come in handy, Cousin," he allowed. "Not too many. We must move furtively."

Sam gave a knowing nod. "I'm accustomed to stealth."

Jack narrowed his eyes. "I'm counting on it. We shall be ghosts."

Chapter Twelve

Evie rode her mare into the rustling woods behind Jack, her thoughts and emotions in tumult. The potential ramifications of his proposed action tumbled through her frazzled mind. Not only was she frustrated with him, but herself. She shared some of the blame for his radical redirection.

Shadows lengthened among the trees with the advancing afternoon. Thickening clouds dimmed the blue peeking between the leafy canopy. The stiff wind had diminished to a light breeze and held the hint of rain in its chill breath.

A welcoming nicker drew her attention to the chestnut colt awaiting their return, his white-streaked face lifted in expectation. Beside him, stood the steady draft horse, Bill. The two friends made a touching scene, but it didn't ease the tempest brewing inside her.

She reined in the mare. Polly was anxious to reunite with her colt and sidled impatiently. Too tired to dismount unaided in these circumstances, she tightened her grip on the horse. Polly tossed her head, wheeling in a circle. The mare was through cooperating, and Evie was fast losing control.

"Jack!" Perhaps a bed of pine needles would cushion her fall if she toppled to the ground.

He swiveled his head at them and sprang from Buck. He stilled Polly with a stern word. The well-trained gelding waited quietly as his master reached up and helped Evie dismount. She slid into his sure grasp, both savoring and resenting his embrace.

He held her to his warm strength. She turned her head, a little awkward in her hat, and rested her cheek against his chest. His coat smelled of wood smoke from countless campfires, horses, and Jack. The dearest scent in the world.

Wild conjectures tumbled in her mind like a rushing stream overwhelming its banks. What if he wasn't here tomorrow? What if he got himself killed? Worse. What if her coming caused his death? He might meet a different end than the one history had in store for him.

Maybe she couldn't alter the fate of someone destined to die. But if that were the case, why had she been sent back?

If he were taken from her, what would she do? Catch the next warble back to the future, leaving behind any hope of a life together? The thought was too terrible to bear.

Unwanted tears blinded her. She blinked and sniffed in a decidedly unladylike manner. "Oh, Jack."

"Don't fret so over me," he whispered.

"What makes you think I am?"

"A hunch." He gently set her aside. "Wait here while I tend the horses and hide our tack. You aren't dressed for physical labor and are dead on your feet."

"True. But—"

"Wait," he insisted.

"Okay." She wouldn't be much use in her restrictive getup, even if she weren't a wreck.

This was an absurd outfit for riding, or anything

else. Crazy what women used to wear. Some modern fashions didn't make much sense either, though. Platform stilettos came to mind. At least she could walk in her riding boots.

Propping herself against a substantial trunk, she looked on blearily while he unsaddled their mounts. If she sank to the earth, she'd never get up, and she wasn't having him haul her back to the house.

"Here." He paused in his brisk movements to pass her the canteen. "Sorry. We are out of food."

"We'll restock." She had finished off the granola bars and he must've eaten the rest of the beef jerky in the black haversack slung over his shoulder. They'd replenish supplies from her carpet bag.

Longing for hot coffee, she sipped metallic mouthfuls as he rubbed down Polly and Buck with a piece of toweling. The aroma of horses and leather mingled with the earthy humus of the woods, comforting scents, and the four animals were glad to be together again. She welcomed the company of horses.

If they had provisions and a tent, she and Jack could camp out here and not have to face the family. Just the two of them, alone…

What now? He fished a small hatchet, reminiscent of a tomahawk, from the waterproof pack he'd tucked beneath an evergreen. "What are you doing?"

"Watch and see."

He deftly hacked boughs from surrounding pines and cedars until he had a pile. After covering the saddles and bridles with a wool blanket, he piled on boughs and further disguised the tack.

She tipped her hand to him. "Clever."

"Have to be," he quipped, with a smile.

Snatching up a wooden bucket, he strode to the barrel filled with water that must have been hauled by wagon from the well, or the nearest stream. He scooped out water and carried a bucketful to each horse, waiting while they drank.

"You shouldn't have to stand around, Jack. You need more buckets or a watering trough up here."

"Will you fashion them?" he asked over his shoulder.

"I wouldn't have a clue how."

"It takes skill and hours we don't have to spare." He lifted a pitchfork and turned his attention to forking hay from the hidden mound. The horses snatched at the fodder he tossed to them.

She eyed the diminishing pile. "More hay needs to be carted up here. A lot more. Easy for me to say, I know. I'm not the one hauling supplies and am dead on my feet. I'm a total wimp."

He flung another forkful to hungry mouths. "Not sure what that is. But you will gain strength after ample rest."

If that could be had.

"Caring for concealed livestock is a lot of work and will only grow when the cows arrive." Pausing, he swiped at his brow. "I reckon they could be driven farther back in the mountains, but several of the older girls will have to remain with them, unless Paul does. And that will take him away."

The enormity of the Wenger's situation weighed on Evie. "Right. What of the sheep and pigs? They can't tether those."

"No. Sheep could also be herded to the mountains. Wish their dog hadn't run off. Bob would be a help."

He swept his hand at the woods. "They might have to let the hogs loose here and attempt to round them up later."

"It will be chaos. And what about the chickens?"

"Same thing," he grunted, flinging another forkful.

She envisioned the resulting confusion. "The Wengers don't have that much livestock in comparison to modern farms. Still, it boggles my mind to think of caring for the animals they do have, while keeping them hidden. Either they find a way to preserve them for the duration of Sheridan's stay, or risk losing every single one down to the last hen."

"It's not right." Mouth set in a tight line, Jack stabbed his fork into the ground and left it. "That's the bulk of the chores done." He resettled his hat and glanced through the trees. "It will be candle-lighting before we know it. Best head back and deliver the news to the family."

"Not *all* of it," she amended. "I'm guessing you will omit your cousin."

"No use in mentioning Sam."

She exhaled heavily. "I can't get over the pair of you being enemies only a few hours ago. How could cousins be so antagonistic to each other? You grew up together."

He stiffened. "That's the nature of civil war, pitting brother against brother. I didn't relish being at odds with Sam and went out of my way not to shoot him."

"That should never even be an option. It's truly a horrendous war."

His shoulders sagged as if under the weight of the fallen. "The worst. And you do not know the half of it."

Frustration roiled in her like a tossing sea. "Then

why do you want to get back in?"

"I don't. Needs must." Eyeing her as he might a skittish mount, he extended his arm. "Come on. Let me help you back."

"I can manage."

Rebuffing his assistance, she picked her way through the trees behind him, while he went ahead, keeping watch. The soldiers shouldn't arrive for a few days, but you never knew. Her long riding habit was a constant battle, and it was the most she could do to stay on her feet. Rocks and roots tripped her up.

"Screw it!" she erupted, yanking her snagged hem from a bush. "I should toss these skirts and just wear my pants."

Too late, she realized her outburst and bit her tongue.

Jack halted at the edge of the woods and turned, a finger to his lips. "What?" he asked under his breath, closing the gap between them.

"I'm not entirely serious," she back-pedaled, in greatly reduced volume. "But…"

"No buts," he said firmly. "You have stunned enough folk today."

"Me? You will floor the Wengers when they learn your plans. Probably shun you—"

"Hold on." He clasped her shoulders, commanding her attention. "They only shun members of their own church, and I'm not Mennonite. And as far as they are concerned, I shall be out on patrol. Which I will be."

"Partly," she interjected.

"I'll monitor the movements of the burning parties," he continued.

"And get yourself shot or strung up in the process."

"Not if I'm cautious." A look of warning crossed his intent expression beneath the wide brim. "It's the bluecoat stragglers who should be worried."

"God help us, Jack. Are you picking them off?"

"How else will word spread not to linger while burning and looting? And I have no doubt they will do both. If we nip at their heels, they may cause less destruction."

"But you will again be the killer you despised."

Indignation flashed in his narrow gaze. "Sheridan is bringing this wrath on himself."

"And if I hadn't told you he was coming and what he intended to do here? Then what? Would you still be off guiding men to safety as you were before my arrival?"

He shook his head. "Not once I discovered Sheridan's true intent. Bringing hard war to the valley is too much to endure without lashing back."

"The Burning is indescribably hateful," she agreed. "But why must you take part in reprisals? Let Sam and the others conduct guerilla attacks. It's right up their alley."

"I am not certain what you mean by that, but they will need me. I excel at being furtive."

"I'll bet." With his instincts, sharp eyes, and knowledge of the landscape, she could well imagine he'd be out in front. Not that this realization brought her any comfort.

He looked long at her. "I know you are deeply vexed, but tell me, truthfully, what would you do if you were me?"

Yearning to guard him welled in her, along with the nagging reminder of her inner workings. "Exactly what you propose," she sighed. "I would resist tooth and nail, and woe unto any man who laid a finger on this place. 'Abandon hope all ye who enter here,' for you are going down."

A smile flickered at his mouth and warmed his eyes. "You cannot attack the soldiers."

She shrugged. "I wouldn't put it past me."

"I don't. And yet you do not wish me to do the same, on a wider scale."

"No. I don't. I want you safe." How could he not see that?

He grew somber. Lines creased his forehead. "With winter around the corner and an army marching our way, survival is the aim. Lessening their fiery blow is the only thing we can do. For come, they will."

An image from a film she'd seen rose in her mind—Irish women dressed in black keening at a funeral. Everything in her wanted to wail. "I don't know why I was sent back at such a time as this. I may alter history, and not for the good."

"The history you shared with me isn't especially admirable. It could use some amending. You came at the right hour, when our valley faces its greatest peril."

Doubt lurked in her soul. "But what if your guerilla actions only succeed in making Sheridan angrier?"

Jack leveled a gaze at her steeped in severity. "I don't think you fully grasp how things are, Evie. I do not lightly choose to ride with Sam. I. Am. Angry."

Chapter Thirteen

Confound it! Evie tripped again, and almost fell. Jack cringed for her amid a flash of annoyance.

Plainly, she was voicing her objection to his plans by refusing his aid and laboring, tearful and exhausted, down the rock-strewn hill. She couldn't expect him to stand by and see the valley torched—not even to keep him 'safe'—and do nothing, could she? How would she ever respect him if he hid while it burned?

He flung his hands up. "Must you be so all-fired mulish?"

She shot him a reproachful glance.

"Evie, you can barely see straight. You are going to sprawl on your face."

Fighting his way through a pitched battle would be easier than dealing with this emotional female. Certainly, she was more difficult than the guerilla tactics he had proposed to undertake. Stealth came naturally to his nature. Admittedly, part of him anticipated reuniting with Sam and routing pockets of torchers. The two cousins would settle their hash.

Despite Jack's efforts to quash his savage side, the warrior in him was still strong. He sighed in frustration. Hadn't Shakespeare said something about being true to 'Thine own self?' Which self? Jack had more than one.

He matched his stride to Evie's faltering steps. "Will you please allow me to assist you?"

"Fine." Chin arched like a duchess, she accepted his arm.

"Thank you." He guided her down the hill, dodging stones, and pondering whether he should speak further with her.

He glanced at her face, so fetching beneath the fashionable hat. And yet, her demeanor was that of a gathering storm. They couldn't arrive at the Wenger's with her in this state, like dry tinder seeking a spark.

Dash it all. He might as well try to converse with her. She was already sorely vexed.

"Evie, I am truly sorry to cause you such distress. But I must defend my homeland as best I'm able. The rest is up to God."

She glared at him. "Don't drag God into this madness. You realize both sides claim Divine aid?"

"Oh, yes. Each soul is welcome to petition the Almighty for his mercy, as do I."

"And I." Challenge sparkled in her unswerving gaze. "What of us, Jack? Are we worth fighting for?"

"Always. I will—am—battling for us. You are everything to me, sweetheart." His feelings for her ran too deep to express.

Her eyes reflected the inner workings of her mind, revealing both her dissent and grudging resolution. "Do what you must. But when I say it's time to follow me to the future, you had better go. We may only have that moment, and that moment alone. I will not ask this of you until it is the only way out, apart from death. I have no idea when it will happen, only that it will."

The depth of her sincerity stuck him, and he detected no flicker of doubt. "You truly believe this, don't you?"

"Yes. I know it makes little sense, but neither does my being here."

"True. You are as unlikely as a rose in winter." The thought sobered him to the core, and he slowly nodded. "I will do as you request. It's a miracle you have come. Another miraculous event may occur."

She appeared slightly mollified. "I pray so, even though we may have altered the timeline of events."

The grassy meadow scent floated on the breeze as he considered. "We cannot know what might have been, unless an account is meticulously chronicled in a volume you can lay your hands on."

"Who can say? My grandmother, maybe, but I can't consult her now."

"No. You must trust your instincts, and what she has taught you." This eccentric woman he'd heard so much about struck him as wise.

Evie pursed her lips for a moment. "You have gone from being a Confederate officer, to a Unionist guide, to what, a Rebel guerilla?"

He shrugged. "I no longer know what I am."

A searching look entered her gaze. "Defender of the Shenandoah? Does that suit you?"

"It's as good a definition as any," he agreed, relieved to find her more amenable. "Am I forgiven for my altered purpose? At heart, I am a Virginian. My loyalty lies here, and always has."

"As does mine," she affirmed, with a hitch in her voice. "I never really thought what it must have been like for the people who lived here in these days, my ancestors among them. I didn't understand what a struggle it was to choose who to fight for, and whether or not to fight at all."

"You don't know what you will do until a thing stares you in the face, as I discovered at Gettysburg. This choice sears me like a flame."

A sheen washed her eyes, as if she understood, and he sensed an unvoiced truce between them. "I will return to you as often as possible amid my forays, under the cover of darkness to avoid detection."

"You must. I will miss you every second," she said, blinking madly.

"As I will you."

"No." She muffled a sniff. "You will be too busy off on your adventures with Sam to give me a thought."

"Never for a moment could I forget you." Throwing caution to the wind, he pulled her to him and wrapped her close, savoring the feel of her in his arms.

They stood in the open. Anyone might look on. They should hasten back to the house, away from watchful eyes.

In a moment. He must make her sure of his love. If not for this impending invasion, he would devote every thought to her.

Gratitude filled him. "Dearest lady. I thank God for his wondrous gift, however you came to be here."

Tucking his fingers under her chin, he tilted her face toward him, and gazed into her streaming eyes. "Don't weep."

Her lips quivered with the effort to stop.

"It will be all right," he soothed.

"Unless it's not."

"Shhh…" He bent his head, covering her tremulous mouth with his certain kiss. Half weeping, she clung to him and returned his tenderness.

Sublime. He didn't mind her tears, and only wished

they were nearer their borrowed bed chamber. He possessed infinite passion, and scant time to show his ardor.

Just as quickly, he chided himself for the unworthy thought. They were not yet wed, though he felt as if he were her lawful husband. If two joined hearts sufficed, then theirs was a holy union, written on his soul.

He reluctantly relinquished her lips. "'These are the times that try men's souls,'" he quoted from Thomas Paine. "Believe me, I would never leave you, if I weren't forced to."

"I will be lost without you," she said in a small voice.

"You will have plenty to do helping the Wengers. And I will be back before you know it."

"Hardly. 'For in a minute there are many days,'" she argued, with a quote from *Romeo and Juliet*.

He prayed that wasn't a prophetic reference.

"I could go with you." She brightened and waved at her riding habit. "Not in this, I'd change."

"Into what? Trousers?"

"Grandma G. also brought me a day dress in the night. Less formal than my other gown," she explained.

Eying her in bemusement, he pointed out the obvious. "No matter what you wear, it's far too risky. Women do not accompany guerilla bands. You would become a legend."

Knowledge welled in her liquid gaze. "And endanger you."

"Endanger us *both*," he stressed. "Get us shot, hung, imprisoned—"

"Very well." Impatience edged the tremor in her voice. "I'll stay behind. Tell me, what do women in this era undertake?"

"With most of the men away, it will fall to them to guard the homestead as best they are able."

She firmed her jaw. "I shall do that. The house is our link, our hope. You speak of survival, Jack. This is ours."

"Then we are dependent on the forbearance of our hosts, to whom we had better return." With their emotions at a sweet simmer rather than a rolling boil, he continued with her across the meadow. "Look." He slowed and nudged her.

A large hole, about four feet deep, had emerged in the side of a bank near the barn. Paul bent near it, hard at work with a shovel. A mound of earth had accumulated where he'd tossed shovelfuls.

Jack stopped with her beside the preoccupied man. "What's this? Are you digging a cave?"

A panting chuckle escaped the worker, and he straightened. His brown coat and wide straw hat blended with the dirt. He paused, resting on his shovel. "I am hurried to make a hideaway for *grumbiere*."

"Potatoes," Jack translated for Evie.

"*Ya*." Paul swept grubby fingers at the garden where the older girls dug tubers and heaped them in sacks. He gestured at the opening he had created. "We will secret the potatoes here. Also, cabbages, carrots, and beetroot and cover them over and under with straw." His lined face creased in a grin. "After we cart away the earth, we will heap cow dung outside the hole to *fernhoodle* the soldiers."

Jack grinned. "No one wants to search in manure. You will fool them." Normally, root vegetables were stored in wooden bins in the cellar, but they would be found there, and he had no doubt every scrap of food would be pilfered by the descending horde.

The foresighted farmer smiled. "Mary and the young ones are squirreling away what they may in the cellar wall, and under the wash house. Stew cooks on the stove. We eat soon, *ya*?"

"Yes." Their innovation impressed Jack.

"Gladly." Evie turned her head to take in the preparations. "You are really being creative."

"We must be." Paul scrutinized them from beneath bushy gray brows. His focus settled on Jack. "What have you learned?"

"It is as we feared. An army is en route and will spread out into the valley in the next few days. You are well advised in your preparations. Be sure to hide your money."

His listener took the news stoically, as was the way with farmers. "We already buried coins under the chicken house to keep them from Rebels," he divulged.

"Ah. Yes." Everyone preyed on the Mennonites, and they were vigilant.

Paul prodded Jack's arm with a mud-streaked finger. "What of you? What will you do?"

Jack chose his words with care. "Help you haul hay and grain to the woods and drive the cows there to conceal them. You may want to herd livestock farther into the mountains. All your animals are in peril. You must decide what is best to do. After I aid you in these preparations, I will go on into hiding, and follow the movements of the burning parties. I shall carry news to you when I'm able."

The older man's sage gaze rested on him. If he guessed Jack's ulterior motive, he didn't say. Finally, he gave a nod. "Have care. If the soldiers catch you, I fear you will not fare well. They do not forgive those who have fought against them, even a man who has redeemed himself as you have done."

"I will be cautious," Jack promised, aware of Evie's solemn silence. "May my wife remain with you while I come and go?"

"She is most welcome to stay. Will you lead more men to the mountains?"

Jack shook his head. "They will have an escort."

His grizzled companion surveyed him quizzically. "How?"

"Don't you see? Anyone wishing to evade conscription into the Confederate Army should seek out the Union troops that will stretch through the valley and follow them north when they leave. Assuming Sheridan ever does." Jack envisioned the Union commander settling in indefinitely.

"He goes," Evie whispered. "In about two weeks."

Good to know. That was a long time to sit on a hot stove, though. A horrific amount of damage could be inflicted in a single day. The slaughter that was Pickett's Charge unfolded in less than an hour. Jack's part in the gory fray took minutes, and he would never ever forget a moment.

Now, what was he undertaking?

He circled his arm around Evie's waist and laid a hand on Paul's shoulder. "Come, my friend. Let's go to the house and sup together while we may. God only knows what lies ahead."

Chapter Fourteen

"The people must be left with nothing but their eyes to weep with." ~General Philip H. Sheridan

Mounted on Buck, Jack surveyed the latest devastation from the top of a hill south of Harrisonburg outside the hamlet of Mt. Crawford. A pall of smoke blackened the sky and smudged the burning landscape. He blinked irritated eyes and muffled a cough. Forewarning of the coming inferno and witnessing the hellish deed firsthand were very different things, and he had followed the burners for several days.

Sam reined in beside him on his red mount. The two cousins could see for miles from this vantage point. It was a sight you never got used to.

"Monster," Jack hissed. "Sheridan wreaks punishment on women and children, the sick and the old…"

Sam's eyes narrowed under the wide-brimmed slouch hat. "I don't consider myself particularly noble, but this—" He waved a gloved hand at the nightmarish scene. "I would never do."

"That's saying a lot," Jack replied through tight lips. "There's plenty you will, and do, carry out."

"But I vowed before you and God to leave the Mennonites alone."

"Be glad you have, or I would break your arm."

"Among other threats," Sam tossed back.

The reprobate didn't seem unduly alarmed by Jack's coercion. But Sam had confined his actions to raiding Union supply lines, disrupting their communications, repossessing stolen horses, spying on and harassing the burners. These activities, which some might find extreme, paled in comparison to the hard war Sheridan wreaked on the hapless civilians.

Jack's thoughts flew to Evie and the Wengers, as they often did. Burning parties, comprised of Union cavalry and infantry, had not yet spread west of Harrisonburg to the farm. But they would. It was only a matter of when. Meanwhile, soldiers spanned out in search of provisions and helped themselves to whatever struck their fancy, and their camps stretched for miles and miles.

This was no mere raid Sheridan was conducting, but the systematic destruction of the Shenandoah Valley. The assault he waged must have been as carefully planned as a military campaign. He'd unleashed his forces in Augusta County, at the southern end of the valley, and had them working their way north, burning as they went. His men followed the Valley Pike, the main artery running through the countryside, and branched off onto adjoining roads.

When the burners finally reached the Wenger's farm, what then? A cold shudder ran through Jack.

He gritted his teeth, determined to ward the torchers off, though he wasn't entirely certain how. For the most part, he, Sam, and the other guerillas endeavored to keep the invaders on the move. In their haste to escape possible retaliation from Rebels lurking in the shadows, the soldiers sometimes overlooked a farm, or didn't burn as thoroughly as they might have if left to act at their leisure. But there were swarms of them in comparison to the furtive few nipping at their heels, and they inflicted a staggering toll.

Like a writhing multi-headed beast, the orange blazes they kindled devoured barns, mills, crops, and anything else thought to be of value to the Confederates. The problem was, these vital resources also sustained the people, some of whom were Unionist sympathizers. Even the folk not inclined to favor the north didn't deserve the fury descending on them. They had nothing to do with the war one way or the other.

If the torchers were extra zealous, they set light to people's homes. From what Jack could gather, Sheridan hadn't ordered the torching of residences, and had instructed his men to leave widows' property alone. But the people were unaware of these stipulations, and hardened men did as they liked, unless an officer intervened and called off the dogs of war.

Homes sometimes caught fire from nearby structures, and caution wasn't necessarily taken to prevent these misfortunes. Residents left with a roof over their heads counted themselves lucky. Others fled the burned-out wreckage of their lives. Sheridan allowed Mennonite and Brethren refugees to attach themselves to his wagon train and accompany his troops. Desperate families flocked to him in want of the most basic means of survival.

The number of wagons in his train swelled like a troubled sea. These refugees would head north with his troops when they left. Each hour his men remained in the land meant more farms and mills set ablaze.

Jack spotted clumps of people below huddled in

yards and fields while bluecoats executed the raging destruction. The cries of mothers and babes carried on the acrid breeze. He knew from experience their pleas would go unheeded. The burners who carried out this vile work had closed their ears.

He'd heard some of the men had refused to take part in the devastation; there were those who hated such ignoble labor. 'This is not the work of soldiers,' they protested. He applauded them, while aware of those willing to take their place.

Gunshots punctuated the hissing crackle. Pigs in their pen toppled to the ground. Cows and sheep were felled where they stood or herded away, bleating and lowing. Whinnying horses were rounded up. These were too valuable to shoot.

Squawking chickens flew. Some dodged the bullets intended for them and hid in brush or trees. Barnyard geese flapped at soldiers, pinching and beating their arms and faces. Men staggered back, and escapees winged to safety. Other birds fell in feathered mounds.

The bloodshed of innocent animals made Jack ill. How silent the valley would be without these familiar companions. He hated their deaths more than the flames, though farmers would be hard pressed to feed any hidden stock with so much fodder destroyed.

A whistle pierced the acrid air from the officer in charge. The shrill note announced the groups' imminent departure from one farm and their movement to the next. The hated piping alerted impending victims to the dreaded visitation as neighbors succumbed to the inferno. Some farmers had herded livestock to the woods beforehand, but many had not received the warning, or there was nowhere to hide.

Jack groaned. "This is a slaughter. We are not doing enough."

Sam blew out his breath. "Not a lot we can do. Never was."

"But every family we ease the toll on even a little will suffer less." Jack sipped water from his canteen, still tasting the ashes in his throat. His whiskey was gone. "Got anything stronger?"

"Here." Sam offered him a swig from the flask in his coat pocket.

He swallowed, relishing the applejack brandy. "Thanks. This is more like it."

"Uh huh." Sam scanned the belching fires and surrounding terrain. "There." He pointed at the clearing near a clump of trees. One of the scouts in their band waved a red kerchief, the signal. "The men are in place. Shall we go and relieve these double-dealers of their coins?"

They had learned several burning parties were working together to fleece their victims, worsening the blow to a hard-hit family. The first group offered to spare the farm in return for the nest egg a farsighted wife might have tucked away. The relieved inhabitants scarcely had opportunity to draw breath before a second group arrived and burned their farm anyway. The accomplices then split the haul between them.

As heinous as this thievery was, Jack wasn't thrilled with Sam's scheme. "I'm not eager for an attack on these parties, unless it's to stop them from continuing their despicable practice. If we are successful, we should return the money to the rightful owners."

"The men won't agree to that," Sam scoffed. "And

how are we to know who it belongs to? A lot of folk have been swindled."

Jack frowned, and restrained Buck, growing restless from the smoke and confusion. "I'm here to help people, not ride with a pack of outlaws."

His affronted cousin straightened in the saddle. "Who are you calling outlaws? If we hinder the bluecoats who are no better than thieves, then so much the better. We have to eat, too, need I remind you? A tidy sum will keep us going for a while."

"Be that as it may, this proposal doesn't sound very high-minded," Jack argued.

Sam waved at the scorching mayhem stretching before them. "Time to live in the real world. You're not off shepherding your flock anymore. Look around you."

"I am," Jack flung back. "What say we send some of these burners on their way?"

"We can do both," his hotheaded relation insisted.

He grunted a reluctant ascent. How had he gotten mixed up with this lawless bunch?

Sam's face hardened. "You know *Twin Oaks* has been sacked?"

His disclosure caught Jack off guard. Reeling from the news, he eyed his kin closely. "Who said?"

"Dunham." Sam named the guerilla waving the kerchief. "He heard from his brother who said *Twin Oaks* is down to the house, alone. Mama sent a team of horses with a wagonload of supplies and several cows to the woods before bluecoats were muddying her floor. She and my sisters hid their jewelry and the silver under the boards, and hams in the attic, but men found plenty to take. And burn. The barn, stable, smokehouse, and every other outbuilding are gone."

"Damn." Jack loved the gracious brick home, shaded by the majestic oaks that gave the house its name. He and Sam had often visited each other while growing up, and *Twin Oaks* was a gem. "I'm sorry. At least the house is standing. There will be a lot of rebuilding after the war."

Sam spat his contempt. "Not without the money to pay for it. As you know dern well."

"I make no argument with that." Confederate notes were worthless and gold dollars coveted. Doubtless, this was what his cousin hoped the soldiers had collected from gullible residents. "I wonder how my father will fare in the coming days? I wish we had parted on better terms."

Sam snorted. "Don't trouble yourself over that conniving Unionist. He will do okay. He's not leaving anything to you, anyway. And my inheritance went up in smoke, so don't scold me for making a dollar here and there."

"Oh, hell. Who am I to judge?" Jack allowed. "But I want to do right by these poor people where we can."

"Yes, Saint Jack."

He gave his cousin a look. A hand raised for emphasis, he continued. "And I haven't seen Evie in days."

"Ah." A knowing glance from Sam firmed their understanding. "Better go after dark if you are paying your bonnie wife a visit."

"That goes without saying."

His cousin waved at the garish scene lighting the sky like a furnace. "I still can't believe she wed you in the middle of this insane war."

"Neither can I." Jack wasn't about to tell him she hadn't. "And it's our honeymoon or would be."

Sam gazed darkly at the fiery desolation below them. "Hell's not a choice destination for wedded bliss."

"And this truly is Hades," Jack lamented. "Our lush land used to be closer to heaven." Wisdom from the great General Stonewall Jackson returned to him. "Jackson said, 'If the valley is lost, Virginia is lost.'"

"When?" Sam asked.

"I don't know. Before he died. A corporal from the Stonewall Brigade told me after Gettysburg."

Sam gave his shoulder a brotherly pat. "Sounds like something Jackson would say."

"And he would be sick at the sight of the valley sinking beneath a mound of ash." Jack could hardly bear it. He gestured at the farm nearest the hill, swarming with bluecoats. "Let's get closer."

He and Sam urged the horses down the track between the trees running along the steep rise. Leaves turning red and gold were interspersed with the green boughs, and the pleasant scent of cedars offset the smoke. They paused in the thicket at its base and peered at the soldiers.

"Look." His animated cousin pointed at the uniformed man in the yard brandishing a flaming stick of kindling he'd snatched from the kitchen hearth. He planned to use this to ignite the barn. "Think I can make the shot?"

Jack weighed the distance with a practiced eye. "Probably. Bet I could."

"Wait your turn." With a wicked grin sparking in his greenish gaze, Sam shouldered the Sharps carbine he'd lifted from a dead Yankee. The red horse remained steady under him as he took aim.

A report rang out, and the stick flew from the offender's grip. The startled man didn't even howl. Sam hadn't left a nick.

Don't kill the burners—unless cornered—was Jack's policy. He preferred intimidation, and Sam usually obliged him. Bluecoats would be furious if they left bodies behind, although resentful Rebels did. As it was, the soldiers scrambled in alarm, scanning in the direction of the shot. Their keen eyes sought the source.

Sam whooped under his breath. "We best head out of here."

"Not quite yet." Jack had his carbine in his grasp.

The rifle rarely let him down. He'd mostly used it for hunting game these past months and hid it in the woods above the Wenger's house when he visited. A second bluecoat gaped in their direction while raising an orange torch. Taking careful aim, he clipped the fiery stick in the man's hand and sent it flying. It was a great shot. One in a thousand, and he silently crowed.

Fearing they were under attack by a sizable force, the soldiers made a mad dash for their horses. That was one farm spared. There would be rejoicing in this home tonight.

"Now, I'm ready to go." He nudged Buck into action.

Chapter Fifteen

Sunset. The last muted rays dipped behind the clouds enfolding the hills. Mist shrouded the dusky meadow, and cold rain pattered Evie's head in the stiff green bonnet Grandma G. had brought her the first night of her journey back in time.

Murkiness surrounded her and Hettie as they picked their way through the slick grass toward the wooded hills. This wasn't a trek anyone wanted to make alone. The sole light came from the lantern in Hettie's hand. The eldest Wenger sister was the same age as Evie and the two had become good friends. It was a relief to have someone to talk to, even though there was much she could not share with the gentle Mennonite girl.

The downfall increased, drumming above their swishing skirts and the soft tread of their laced shoes. The seeping wet penetrated everything. More than a nip of fall chilled the air, and Evie shivered in her green wool cloak.

A soft brown bonnet, like the kind the women wore on *Little House in the Prairie,* covered Hettie's white-capped head and she hugged a homespun nut-brown cloak. Doubtless, she was also cold, but used to discomfort. Nineteenth century farm life was never easy, and the war had made it that much more difficult. Sadly, harsher trials lay ahead.

How indulged Evie had been in comparison, and she was no slacker. She'd soon harden up. Had to. "Has it been less than two weeks since my arrival?" That hardly seemed possible.

"*Ya*," Hettie affirmed.

"Feels like a life time." Keeping her next query to herself, she pondered what Grandma G. was telling friends and family about her sudden disappearance.

The inventive woman probably spun a plausible tale, without divulging the truth. Maybe she simply said Evie was off riding, posing for pictures, leading garden tours, or helping in the shop as she usually did, and 'unavailable for comment' or some excuse such as a press secretary might give.

What about her cell phone? Normally, she answered text messages as soon as she could. Not now. And she'd vanished from social media. That might not be such a bad thing, but it wasn't like her.

Perhaps Grandma G. said she'd lost her phone. That wouldn't fly. Everyone knew she'd soon have another.

She hoped no one was frantic about her welfare and had no idea how long she would remain in this era. Memories of the home and life she'd known ran through her consciousness in an ever-present stream. She missed her family. Most of all, she missed Jack. His absence was an aching void, and her thoughts of him formed a constant prayer, like a bridge to heaven.

Her less formal yellow-checked gown had seen a lot of work since his departure and was her only suitable dress for labor. She smoothed the rosy gold brooch closing the high neckline. The jewelry came from her great-great-great grandmother, who, strangely enough, was alive in the southern end of the valley right now. If a bluecoat demanded the brooch from Evie, as had happened to her spunky ancestor during The Burning, she would also stab him in the thumb with the pin and preserve it.

Weird, to think of the jewelry being in two places at once. Everything about time travel was bizarre.

She dropped her gaze to the brave little light guiding them across the field. Hettie held the black painted tin lamp by its narrow semicircular handle. The glass front emitted the glow from the candle secured within, one of Paul's handicrafts. Without the wavering beam, they couldn't see to make these late evening excursions to feed and water the horses in the woods behind the house. They also scattered grain for the chickens and hogs loosed among the trees to keep the animals fed and returning to a given spot. Thick grass disguised the uneven ground, and Evie cautiously placed each step. "Too bad we don't have an oil lamp. It would better light our way."

The wide brim of Hettie's bonnet bobbed in a nod. "There is little oil to be had since the Union blockade."

"Right. Of course." Evie kept forgetting the dratted blockade. Unless something was grown or fashioned by hand, it was in short supply, and substitutes made. She bet no one else forgot this grinding fact. Hettie must think she'd lost it.

She took the conversation in a different track. "I wish we could come up here during the day."

Hettie loosed a small sigh. "Someday, soon, we hope."

Because foraging soldiers might spot and follow them in daylight, and steal the horses, they waited until evening to venture forth. Bluecoats didn't stray far from camp after dark, with good reason. Stealthy guerillas dogged their every step. Or might. They never knew.

Evie remembered her father telling her Sheridan lost patience with the Rebels shadowing his troops and sniping at the burners.

Seriously? Did the arrogant general really think valley men would welcome his army with open arms when they came to wreak destruction?

Jeeze. If Evie invaded another land, she would anticipate considerable resistance. Men were crazy, and war was hideous, this one especially so. She felt as if it would never end, and she'd only experienced it for a week.

She tucked chilled fingers inside her cloak. "Maybe Jack will come tonight."

"That would gladden your heart," Hettie said softly.

"I live for his visits." She hadn't seen him in what seemed like ages. She ducked her head in the bonnet. "I'm sure he would come if he could."

"The valley burns." Hettie's quiet tone was grave.

"I can smell it." Even in the cold rain, the tinge of smoke reached them, and not only from the kitchen hearth.

Mary couldn't cook during the day as the savory aroma drew hungry soldiers. The annoyed woman cooked and baked at night, and that's when the family ate. They snuck snacks of cold food in the day. Evie hid her private stash in the attic along with her spare clothes and the carpet bag. She'd removed and burned the food wrappers, so no one would wonder at the plastic or the dates stamped on the labels. She reserved most of her supplies for Jack, but also shared some with the Wengers.

"The smoke is always with us." Hettie's hand shook from cold, or apprehension. Consequently, the candle in her lantern wobbled, and the little light wavered. "The stench will only worsen as the burners draw near. I dread to see the flames."

Trepidation washed over Evie. "As do I. Jack may have word of their movements."

For a long moment, Hettie did not reply. "He is not only following the soldiers, is he?"

Evie hesitated, then decided to reveal part of the truth. "He urges them along, so they do not linger at their evil work. Please do not confide this to your parents, or anyone."

"I will not speak of it. He is a good friend to us. *Sie Batt nemme duhn ich gern*, I will willingly take his part," she translated.

"Thank you." With the secret tucked between them, they walked on toward the inky trees. "I worry about him," Evie further confided. "I shudder to think of him getting shot. Worse—hung. He might recover from a gunshot."

"*Ya*. I have helped nurse wounded men. But there is much loss of limbs with these injuries and risk of infection. Soldiers must not catch him here."

"No. He will only come after dark and leave before dawn." A shiver of anticipation ran through her. "Maybe tonight…"

"Maybe…" Wistfulness hinted in Hettie's reply.

Guilt pricked Evie. The girl could not be blamed for having a crush on this handsome, deeply torn, young man. Even though the soft-spoken Mennonite and the adventurer never really had a future together. Hettie couldn't know Jack's heart belonged to Evie even before they met. No one had.

Her conscience chided her for keeping the bedroom to herself on the chance he might visit. Was it right to hog that space, while the sisters crammed together?

The Wengers had insisted the newlyweds have privacy on the rare occasions when he returned. The rest of the time, he camped with Sam and the men in his band. What was Evie to do, confess all? That would be too much for the family to bear. Besides, she would marry him the instant they had the chance. As far as everyone else was concerned, she already had.

If for some reason she never made it back to the future, then he was her husband, and that was that. In return for the hospitality shown them, she tried to be of use to the family. She aided them in hiding food and helped with the chores, more difficult since Paul was away. He'd shouldered a pack of supplies in a bedroll and herded the cows and sheep to the mountains. The farm dog, Bob, a collie mix, had reappeared and gone with him. The families' joy at Bob's coming convinced her he must herd like a pro.

"*Gott segen eich.* God bless you. I pray you and Jack will soon be reunited," Hettie graciously offered. "Lord willing, we shall gather our animals and return them home before long."

"Amen." Evie continually petitioned God. "But I fear the worst is yet to come." In fact, she knew it.

Hettie winced, and bent toward her. They were about the same height and their bonnets touched. "I do not know what we shall do if the house is burned."

Neither did Evie, and with greater cause for fear, as

it was her portal to the future. "I will not let the soldiers burn it."

Even in the limited light, she was aware of Hettie gaping at her. "How will you stop them? They are deaf to pleas."

"I do not have a plan, but I will try. I was not raised Mennonite. It may get violent."

"You will fight them?" Amazement resounded in the girl's query.

"Maybe. And yell at them to go away."

"You are stout-hearted, Evie. But I fear for you."

"I fear more what Jack may do if he is here when they come. He was once a soldier and would defend you."

Her confidante inhaled sharply. "He cannot be here then. He must hide."

"I agree. But Jack has a destiny in this house," Evie disclosed.

"Does he?"

"As do I." Though she did not fully grasp her role in altering his fate, only that a way would reveal itself.

"How wondrous." Her listener was slack-jawed.

"I'm sorry. I guess that doesn't make much sense." She had revealed too much.

Hettie touched her shoulder. "I see you feel a part of our home. This is good. But our path is not the way of bloodshed. The church forbids violence, as that could result in the loss of life. Jack understands this."

"Yes, he does. But knowing a thing and acting on it are very different matters."

"Then we must pray he does not forget."

"This quandary also causes turmoil in my heart." And Evie might be worse than Jack when the burners came.

"If you think to battle the soldiers, then yes." Hettie sounded bemused.

There was more. Much more. But how could Evie explain something this fantastical?

She also needed Jack to remember his promise to go with her when she asked. Everything was at stake. His life, their future together… It was difficult to say what anyone might do. Hettie had no idea how entangled the past, present, and future were for them. Should she tell her? Did she dare?

Rain whispered around them. They were alone. No one else could overhear.

"There is something you should know about me…" Evie began, trailing off. The light revealed only a glimpse of Hettie's face beneath the bonnet. She could not be certain of the expression in her blue gaze.

Rather than confide her true origins, Evie swerved in another direction. "My family are from Augusta County. The McIntyre's." She doubted a Mennonite would be acquainted with Scot's-Irish Presbyterians in a neighboring county, and the Wengers had not pressed for details about her background. They probably suspected something was off there.

Hettie seemed puzzled by this seemingly random revelation. "You do not often see them?"

"No." How could she explain that this generation of McIntyre's had never seen her in their lives?

"You prefer to remain here with us?"

"Very much, but…" Again, she faltered.

"What of your grandmother? Do you see her?"

"Usually. She is…" Evie could hardly say 'here' only in the future.

"Nearer?" Hettie supplied.

"Yes. But I cannot stay with her now."

"Ah. The war," her companion concluded.

"Yes." A good excuse, and possibly the truth. The war did lie behind her travel to the past. She had been brought back for this time and place.

She badly wanted Hettie to understand but would likely only persuade the poor girl that she belonged in a mental institution. This would leave Hettie with the choice of protecting Evie from herself or confessing her mental ills to Paul and Mary. An impossible situation to place this gentle soul in. Some things were better left unsaid.

They continued in the pattering silence, enveloped in misty dark rain. If only she could put an invisibility spell around the farm and hide it from the coming soldiers.

****

Shivering in her chemise, the lacy pink wrap thrown over her shoulders, Evie knelt near the opening in her floor. A candle on the bedside stand illuminated her room on this rainy night. Her actions might seem peculiar, but the only way she could think to keep her grandmother apprised of her situation was to make entries in the small brown diary the wise woman had stuck in the carpet bag.

The slim volume smelled of leather, and Grandma G. had included an ink pen. Perhaps, she had meant for Evie to communicate this way. After all, they shared the same home, only in alternative time periods.

Each evening, Evie noted the date and jotted a brief entry. After recording her account, she hid the journal under the section of loose boards in the floor. The brown and tan striped rug concealed this hiding place now, but if Grandma G. searched beneath the Oriental carpet in the modern-day version of this room, she might find the diary. The space in the floor had existed for as long as Evie could remember.

Today's entry read: *October Third, Eighteen Sixty-Four. No sign of the burners yet, but smoke drifts in the air like a distant forest fire. I fear they will come soon. We are as prepared as possible. Jack is away with the guerillas. He is in my thoughts every moment. Hettie is my friend, but I cannot tell her about myself as I would like. I wish I could do more for her, for them all. I love you, Grandma G. Give everyone a hug for me. ~Evie*

She fastened the narrow strap around the journal, slid the pen in place, and put the leather volume back beneath the boards. Rather like leaving a message in a bottle. Maybe Grandma G. would discover her attempt at communication. She was clever enough to look.

Getting word to or from Jack was impossible. Evie didn't know where in the valley he was. She pictured him shadowing Yankees, riding through the trees, and hunched around a woodsy campfire with Sam and the others. Bluecoats would never find them there, not with their fear of ambush.

She straightened, snugged her shawl more tightly around her, and tiptoed in her stocking feet to the window. Her white cotton chemise hung below her knees. Lace edged the capped sleeves and drawstring neckline. Lacking anything else, she slept in this. Tonight, she'd need the lacy wrap under the blankets, too. The chilly room had no heat.

Members of the household were still, tossing anxiously in their beds, maybe, but quiet. The younger girls slept with their mother while Paul was away. The remaining sisters had each other. Evie, the supposed married lady, was alone and restless.

Peering through the glass, she strained for sight of Jack in the yard. There was no reason to expect him, apart from hope. She couldn't see him in the foggy blackness, anyway. Still, she looked. This waiting would drive her crazy.

She took the brush from the stand and ran the bristles through her hair. Keeping the long lengths and the rest of her remotely near her usual hygienic standards was a major challenge. Sponge baths were routine. Sinking her entire self into the tub took too many heated buckets of water and trips up the stairs. She'd washed her hair in tepid water, thankful for the lavender shampoo and soap in her bag. She shared her extra bar with the others. They were awed.

Each evening, she sponged the worst of the grime from her dress and hung it over the stair railing to dry. She had never gone this long without a decent change of clothes. At least, she had extra bloomers and washed them thoroughly. The riding habit or the full gown from her first night weren't suited to work, but she would have to wear one of them while she gave her day dress a good scrubbing.

This was her life now, while she waited for...

"Jack?"

Her heart leapt in her chest as, holding a finger to his lips, he crept in her door.

Chapter Sixteen

Seeing Evie poised by the window held Jack transfixed. She wore only the simple white chemise and lacy wrap, her glorious hair tumbled about her feminine curves. The tantalizing whiff of lavender hung in her chamber. She seemed a dream. He could pinch himself.

No need. He was awake. Of that, he was sure. Many times, he'd flown back to her in his sleep. This was real.

Outside, foggy rain enclosed the silent household and the farm. Southeast of Harrisonburg, cinders engulfed his singed valley. Her beauty made vibrant contrast to the ugliness he'd witnessed. Worse than anything he'd seen yet.

Sunk in the winter of his soul, he'd been mired down by death and destruction. She transcended the anger and pain churning inside him, drawing him to something infinitely better. She wasn't only a bonnie woman, she was Evie, his brightest star, glowing before him in purity and light. At this moment, he declared her an angel.

"I almost didn't believe it possible," he said, his voice raw with emotion and the lingering effects of smoke.

Her forehead creased. "What?"

"You, dearest lady. A vision for sore eyes, standing before me like a fresh spring morn."

The flickering candle revealed her tremulous smile and the glad hope in her face. Tears sparkled in her eyes. Her shining gaze riveted on him, as if he were the answer to her prayers. And the certainty came to him. He was.

"I'm here, where you left me. I feared you wouldn't return," she whispered.

He surveyed her in wonder. "How did I ever leave you in the first place? How can I go again?"

She shook her head at him. "Don't."

"With all my heart, I wish I could stay. But I must be away before dawn. Or hide Buck in the woods and myself in the attic."

She firmed the quiver in her chin. "That's not safe with the soldiers closing in."

"Not especially. Nowhere is. I am ever on the move in the day." He tossed his hat on the chair. "I bedded Buck in the barn for the night. Stowed my bedroll and carbine out of sight, then I came in search of you."

"What is happening out there? We can smell the hint of smoke but have seen nothing."

His jaw clenched. He hung the black haversack from the back of the chair. "The burners are busy. I fear I have no good tidings to deliver," he said, apologetically, unbuckling his leather belt and laying it and his holstered revolver on the seat. "Sam and I did little to lessen the hellish fate descending on the people. We cannot halt the rolling blue tide but brought small mercies to a few farms."

"You did what you could. I hold nothing against you for trying, Jack."

He smiled through the sting of regret and

frustration hounding him. "Thank you for saying that."

"I could say much more. You are enough for me. You are everything."

"As you are to me. I truly mean it. To my core." He strode noiselessly over the boards, covering the distance between them in a heartbeat.

Clasping her hands in his, he held them to his lips, kissing each dear knuckle. Her fingers were reddened since he last saw her. "You have worked hard in my absence."

She nodded. "Grandma G. would be proud."

"As am I." He pressed a kiss to her callused palms. "If I hadn't already proposed to you, I would ask you to wed me."

Her answering smile promised the reply he craved. "And I would say yes again. But if the opportunity to marry never comes, then I am your wife, now and forever."

He could weep with joy and battled not to be overcome by the bittersweet sensation flooding him. The bitter edge was because of the limit to their time together, the bounding sweetness because they had this precious moment.

"You make me supremely happy," he managed past the lump in his throat.

Her expressive eyes brimmed with a wealth of feeling. "As you do, me. Happiness is not easily come by amid The Burning."

"No." He cupped his roughened hands to her smooth cheeks. "We are the more miraculous for it."

She covered his fingers with hers. "We are."

Arching on her stocking feet, she brought his lips to hers in a kiss swollen with tenderness. He returned the rapturous press on his mouth in unspeakable gratitude that she was here. So many had fallen of illness, injury, and want. Countless others would succumb before this brutal war ended.

Were he and Evie assured of anything beyond this hour, when even that was incredible? She spoke of a future together in some distant realm, but he only grasped *now*.

Kissing her harder, he caught her in his arms and held her close to him, slowly circling with her in the room. They might be dancing, the weathered scout, beaten down by strife, and the lovely lady, lost in a waltz, swirling to the ancient melody of couples in love. No music was needed, only their panted breaths against the falling rain.

How long they remained like this with her clasped in his embrace, their heated lips pressed together, he couldn't say.

Pausing by the bed, he gently laid her on the mattress. Should he step away and stretch himself on the cot? He searched her eyes. "Shall I stay with you tonight?"

"Need you ask?" she chided, in mock scolding.

He bent near, smoothing a caramel streaked tendril at her cheek. "Yes. I am a gentleman."

"For all intents and purposes, you are my husband. Your place is at my side."

"The most profound utterance," he assured her, basking in the wonder of her declaration. "I suppose God knows."

"No *suppose* about it. Of course, God does. Who do you think brought us together?"

He almost said, 'Your grandmother.' Instead, he

answered, "I'm not one to argue with the Almighty. Especially not when God and I are in accord."

She smiled. "Well then?"

"I would scramble to you in an instant, but I am fully dressed." Only his coat was open down the front.

Dropping his hand from her face, he straightened and peeled the outer garment from his shoulders. The nearest he'd come to a bath was a dunk in an icy stream.

He folded his coat over the chair. "Sorry, sweetheart. I reek of smoke, and days in the saddle."

She propped her head on an elbow. "I don't mind that you do, though I resent the cause of your trials."

"Sheridan?" he clarified.

"Who else?" she sighed.

He unbuttoned his vest, adding it to the growing pile, and turned toward her. "General Grant, maybe. Likely his orders lie behind Sheridan's fiery visitation."

She lifted one shoulder and let it drop. "Six of one, half a dozen of the other."

"What?" At times, she made no sense.

"Something Grandma G. says. Both men are responsible."

"Ah. No doubt." Stark images haunted Jack.

He swiped the back of his sleeve over his eyes as if to banish them. "The things I've seen, Evie. Some I cannot forget. I have blood on my hands, too, but not like this. One officer ordered a foal shot. It was too young to follow its mother. Like Polly's colt."

She gasped, raking at her hair. "Could he not leave the poor baby be?"

"With rare exceptions, the bluecoats leave nothing. The animals go with them or are slaughtered."

"Who does such a thing?" she asked, in sorrowing disbelief.

"Men who have lost all humanity." He eyed her through his hurt, like a wounded animal. A tear slid down his cheek, and he blinked at more. "What have the people done to deserve such punishment?"

"Nothing, Jack. They are in the wrong place at the wrong time. That is all. Someday, the valley will be beautiful again. I promise."

"I pray so."

"Trust me," she soothed, reaching out to him. "Come here. Let us make it as right between us as we can. And know I will love you forever."

He slid into her arms. "I believe you will. And my heart is yours."

****

A rap on the downstairs door roused Jack from a dreamless slumber. More content than he had been in years, or ever, he lay with Evie entwined in his arms. He cracked an eye at the window. The palest light of earliest dawn silvered the sky in the thick haze lingering from last night's rain.

Realization came. He could kick himself. He'd overslept and meant to be away by this hour, but the thick fog would conceal his movements for a while yet.

Again, the insistent knock.

Evie stirred drowsily against him. "Who's that?"

"Not soldiers," he whispered, brushing a kiss to her creamy shoulder. "They don't knock. I will go and see."

She turned her head toward the window and tensed. Her shadowed gaze returned to him. "We weren't expecting anyone to call at this hour."

He clasped her hand. "Don't worry. It's probably

just a neighbor with news."

"Before sunrise, in heavy fog? Be careful."

"Yes." He nodded his awareness of the need for caution and pressed a quick kiss to her mouth.

If only he could linger here with her. What bliss that would be.

Loathe to part from her sweet warmth, he sat upright in bed. Accustomed to hurried dressing, he pulled on his clothes, fastened buttons, adjusted his suspenders, and tugged on his boots in rapid movements. The warrior in him conjectured where he'd left his carbine—in a slit between the stones at the base of the barn, too far for him to immediately retrieve.

He lifted the holstered revolver on his leather belt and fastened the buckle at his waist. His coat concealed the loaded gun. Uppermost in his mind, was the silent vow he'd made not to fire in this pacifist home, or on the farm, if he could possibly avoid it. Still, he had the weapon if needed. No bluecoats were taking him.

With a wistful glance at Evie, seated in bed clutching the blankets to her bare skin, he strode across the room and out the door. He encountered Mary Wenger in the dusky hall. She'd thrown a gray shawl around her plain white nightgown and wore a white cap. The candle dancing in the black iron holder she held revealed the apprehension in her lined face. The younger girls peeped anxiously from behind their mother.

Mary relaxed visibly upon seeing him. "Thank God you have come, Jack. Paul's away and I have no notion who might be calling. We cannot be too careful with looters afoot."

"No." He doubted they'd knock either and patted

her thin shoulder reassuringly. "Wait here."

With the feminine household hanging on his every step, he hastened down the stairs. Keeping a hand at his waist, he crept to the door. The predawn light was dim and the mist too thick for a glance out the window to offer any insight, or forewarning, if that were wanted.

He turned the lock and cracked the door, widening it at the sight that greeted him. The young Rebel called Dunham, the signature red scarf at his neck, supported Jack's reprobate cousin. His normally high-spirited relation sagged against the fellow guerrilla. Blood painted a path down Sam's coat sleeve, and he clasped a crimson-stained glove to his upper arm.

"What happened, Cousin?" Jack hissed.

"Got shot, didn't I?" he said between gritted teeth. "Yankee sentries. We strayed too close."

A vision of mounted soldiers pounding up the lane sharpened Jack's alarm. "Were you followed?"

"No. We escaped in the fog."

Dunham's brown eyes creased beneath his wide-brimmed black slouch hat. "Sam said you would be here and I should bring him. But this is a Unionist household?"

Jack bent nearer. "It makes no difference. Mennonites will help anyone in need."

Dunham seemed dubious. "I heard something of the sort. Didn't believe it."

"Believe, and come in quickly, before you're both seen." Jack motioned them forward, stepping aside to make room. The instant they were through the door, he closed it, and turned the lock. "Where did you leave your mounts?"

"The barn." Dunham looked none too easy about it.

"They should be all right for the moment." Jack shifted his cousin, wincing, into his support. Like him, Sam was a lanky man, and Dunham had a slight, wiry build. The loyal friend had done a lot to support Sam this far, especially as he couldn't bear weight on one leg.

"Why are you limping?" Jack scanned him for telltale blood.

"Twisted my ankle getting off the horse. Nothing compared to—" Sam broke off with a groan.

"Mary," Jack summoned over his shoulder. "A bullet wound needs tending down here."

"*Ach.* That is bad," she answered from the upstairs landing.

"Could be worse. It's his arm."

Bullets striking the chest or abdomen nearly always proved fatal. The Minie´ balls commonly fired from rifled muskets often inflicted severe internal damage. Limbs might require amputation. Jack wasn't certain what ball had stuck Sam and prayed he wouldn't lose his arm. If the worse came, they would have to find a doctor. Mary couldn't perform the gruesome surgery.

"Be aware, it's Sam Hobbs," he disclosed to her, and all other ears privy to their exchange.

"Ach," she repeated, a waver in her tone.

"He's my cousin," Jack added.

"Ich bin om cooma." She slipped into German in her nervousness, while declaring her intention to come.

Sam's lamentable reputation preceded him. Even so, Jack trusted Christian charity, not the memory of his cousin's derisive attitude and pilfering behavior, would guide Mary's actions. She and her family were forgiving souls.

"I'm coming, too." Hettie's assurance carried down the steps.

"Thank you." Jack knew she was an able nurse.

"I don't know how much help I will be but I'm on my way," Evie called softly.

The women's immediate response was gratifying. "Good. We can use all the hands we can get."

Quick footfalls followed overhead. Drawers opened and closed. A wardrobe door creaked. The household buzzed as the women and girls dressed.

What should they do with Sam? He wasn't in a fit state to go far. Daylight would soon be upon them. Burning parties hadn't yet reached the country west of Harrisonburg, but foragers might appear at any hour.

Jack considered the parlor. "Not the couch. We'll stain it, and there isn't inadequate room to work. Let's take him to the kitchen."

Together, he and Dunham eased the groaning man across the floor and into the coziest room in the house. Jack indicated the table, built long to seat the large family. "How about that? It's the best makeshift spot for surgery."

"Not there," Sam objected.

"Sorry, Cousin. Nothing else for it."

Dunham lent his assistance and they carefully heaved the patient onto the clean oak surface. Jack set Sam's gray hat aside and eased a folded towel under his head.

"Stir up the fire and add kindling," he directed Dunham. "We need warm water. That, alone, shouldn't draw scavengers like the scent of breakfast."

"I sure hope not. We're sitting ducks in here." Dunham turned his somber attention to the cast iron stove dominating that side of the room.

"There's a hiding place in the attic if need be," Jack divulged.

Sam's eyes glinted in triumph. "I knew it. Not that it matters a lick now." He'd promised Jack his days of hunting down army evaders and deserters were over.

Dunham brightened a little. "It matters if we need to scuttle up there." He soon had wood crackling in the stove.

What a pity they didn't dare risk cooking a proper breakfast. Jack could do with one, and imagined everyone else could, too. The guerrillas were on slim rations, unless they raided Union supplies, then they ate heartily. That's probably what Sam and Dunham were attempting when they were detected.

Mary swept into the kitchen, seeming more confident with an injury to see to. In her arms were a gray wool blanket and strips of linen. Her gaze fell on Sam, and she pursed her lips, then shifted her focus to the newcomer at the stove.

"Mister Dunham Owens, Mrs. Mary Wenger," Jack said, by way of introduction.

The young Rebel tipped his hat to her. "Ma'am."

"Mister Owens." She returned her attention to the man grimacing on the table. "We will do our best for you, Mister Hobbs. You need to get his coat and shirt off, Jack, or cut the cloth from him."

"I hate to do that. What's he to wear? Need your help, Dunham." Against Sam's cries, the two men gingerly peeled the blood-soaked garments from him and piled them on the floor.

Jack studied the ugly hole in the fleshy part of his arm below the shoulder. If he were fortunate, the bullet hadn't fractured a bone. No fragments were visible, but it was hard to tell with the blood.

Mary pressed a folded linen square to the wound to stem the flow. Tremors ran through Sam's lean muscled form. Was he reacting to the shock of the injury or taking a chill? Or both?

The matron took charge. "Hold this, Jack."

He slid his hand over the cloth in place of hers, and she briskly covered Sam with the blanket, leaving only his injured arm exposed. "Hettie?" she summoned.

"Here, Mama." Her eldest daughter appeared at her elbow, blue eyes creased in concentration.

Hettie nodded at Dunham, cast a pitying glance at Sam, and gathered the stained mound of laundry. "I will put these to soak in the wash tub and get the yarrow."

"*Ya. Gut.*" Mary affirmed her herb choice. "We will also steep the leaves to make medicinal water. The crushed leaves and root are used to dull pain and heal wounds, Mister Hobbs."

"I'm beholden to you, ma'am," he ground out. "It's more than I deserve."

Her steady regard did not falter. "The Lord desires mercy."

He met her gaze through pain-glazed eyes. "Not many follow God's wishes these days."

"We do in this house, as best we are able."

Jack could humbly vouch for that. His conscience smote him. How could he possibly consider a shootout of any kind on this farm? Hadn't the Wengers taught him better? If bluecoats came, then he and the other two must hide or face capture, and execution for guerillas was more likely than imprisonment.

Mary gestured at Dunham. "Have you any spirits

for Mister Hobbs?"

"Applejack brandy, ma'am." He drew a glass flask bottle from his black coat pocket, partly filled with amber fluid. "Sam's had a goodly draught."

"Best give him another. The brandy will warm him, and he has need of it. We have no laudanum. I will heat the water."

The little woman darted away like a busy wren. She took an iron kettle from the walnut cupboard bearing cups, bowls, plates, and other kitchen stuff. The best goods had been hidden but cooking day-to-day with nothing on hand was impossible. She flew out the door to the rain barrel on the stoop, reappeared almost immediately, and set the kettle on the hot stove to boil.

Evie's warm voice carried from the parlor where Jack expected the sisters had gathered. He imagined their frightened faces, and her heartening presence. "Here you go, girls. There's plenty for everyone, including our guests. I brought pretzels, oatmeal-nut bars, dried fruit, and chocolate—"

Small squeals of delight disrupted her. "Chocolate?" they queried in unison.

"From my generous grandmother. I have been saving it, and this is the day."

The dear girl must have dug deep into her carpet bag. He suspected she had been reserving the food stuff for him.

"Eat up," she encouraged. "I will make us all some instant coffee, as soon as I'm able. A special treat."

On the tail of her joyously received gifts and promise of more, Evie sailed into the kitchen. She wore the yellow-checked gown, her bountiful hair loosely pinned on her head and tied with a yellow ribbon. She held an embroidered pillow case filled with goodies, reminiscent of Santa's pack.

She took in the assembly and smiled at Jack, like sunshine streaming into darkness, then hastened to the table. No shyness was evident as she greeted Dunham. "Hello. I'm Evie Ramsey."

"Pleased to meet you, ma'am." He gaped at her while parting with more of his precious brandy to Sam. He supported the injured man's head with one hand and administered sips with the other. "You say all the supplies in that bag came from your grandmother, even coffee and chocolate?"

"Yes. I also have some sugar."

Dunham gave a low whistle. "She must be acquainted with a wily blockade runner and pay him in gold."

"Maybe so. I took much for granted before coming here." Evie dropped her gaze to Sam. "I'm very sorry for your injury and brought some things I hope may help."

His lips curved in the ghost of a smile despite his gritted teeth. "Most kind, ma'am."

"Please, call me Evie. We are family now. Besides, we met, remember?"

He coughed on a swallow. "We did, indeed."

If Sam were his normal self, he would thoroughly enjoy this exchange. But he wasn't. Before Evie tired him, Mary skirted to her side, a question in her brown eyes.

"What have you brought us?"

"A lot of food, and…" Evie fished in her bag and held out what appeared to be tweezers and a small metal tool with a hook on the end. "It's a crochet hook, in case you need to probe the wound. Might these tweezers clamp the bullet?"

Wearing a perplexed expression, Mary took the items and examined them. "This may serve," she said, referring to the crochet hook. "The tweezers are too short. I have what you call a bullet extractor."

Jack had heard of the medical instrument found on a local battlefield and given to the prominent healer in the area.

"Wow. Okay." Evie restored the tweezers. "I also brought some medication to lessen his pain." She opened her palm to reveal two white pills. "This helps me when I take it."

'For cramps,' she added under her breath. But he supposed pain was pain.

Mary bobbed her approval and Evie handed the medicine to Dunham. "Give him these with the brandy."

The ready assistant gave Sam the pills.

She dipped back into her bag and removed a small, strangely marked bottle containing a foreign substance. "Hand sanitizer so we don't spread germs to the wound."

What on earth? Everyone, including Jack, stared at her.

"Never mind." Her cheeks pinkened and she tucked away her offering.

Whatever it was, must remain a mystery at present. She set her bag on the dry sink attached to the cupboard. "Eat whatever you like. I brought plenty."

Mary nodded graciously. "Most welcome."

"A taste of glory land." Jack's mouth watered at a delectable sniff of the storehouse, but he stayed with

Sam and the compress. "I'll get my share in a bit, thanks."

Dunham pocketed his depleted flask and headed toward the stash. "I'll save you both a morsel."

"You had better leave more than that," Jack warned. Dunham wasn't a big fellow, but he could put away the food.

The back door opened, and Hettie blew in with the early morning breeze. Sunshine was breaking through the mist. So much for concealment. Jack and the others must remain indoors until evening. Maybe longer.

His focus returned to the fresh-faced girl gripping a stoneware bowl the same shade as her simple brown gown. Coppery reddish hair peeked from under her white cap. An herbal pungency accompanied her entrance. Feathery green leaves and pounded root filled the vessel she set on a stool.

Taking the kettle from the stove, she poured steaming water over the aromatic plant, except for the piece of pulverized root she reserved. This, she carried to the table.

She stopped by Jack, her clear blue eyes seeking Sam.

"Yarrow root dulls the pain, sir. I will place this on your wound and leave it a while, then sponge your arm with the herbal water."

He regarded her intently and inclined his head. "That sure sounds better than nothing to numb it."

Dunham also seemed impressed by the herbalist. "Much," he agreed between squelchy bites of chocolate.

"I can testify to the healing skills in this house." Jack nodded at Hettie. "I am ready when you are."

"Now," she directed, and he lifted the stained cloth he'd held in place.

She spread the pounded root over the oozing hole in Sam's upper arm, her light touch eliciting only a slight grimace. "We will wait for it to work. Please restore the cloth, Jack." She turned enthusiastically to Evie. "I overheard the excitement in the garden. What did you bring?"

"All sorts of things. Are you hungry?"

"Oh, yes. Everyone is."

"I can make coffee with the instant brew," Evie offered. "I even have cream and sugar."

"Your grandmother is a true saint." Hettie waved at the kettle. "We need more boiling water."

"I will refill the kettle." Mary still puzzled over the crochet hook Evie had given her. "How did you know this might be useful? Have you looked on as a bullet was removed?"

"Not exactly. I have watched medical programs, like plays," she said, the struggle to explain in her face.

Plays? People made entertainment about bullet removal? What was in this future she spoke of? Jack wondered.

He had no idea. His ears were tuned for the faintest hint of drumming hooves and boots in the yard.

Chapter Seventeen

Where was Jack? Had he run into blue-clad soldiers?

Evie's knees ached from kneeling on the floorboards in front of the attic window. Still, she stayed and stared at the malevolent blackness blotting out the stars. Prayers for his safety repeated in her troubled mind like a soundtrack. He and Dunham had ridden off at sunset to learn news of the violent increase in smoke.

The acrid fog had worsened all day, snaking through the chinks in the house. She no longer thought of it as a whiff on the breeze. The stench dominated every breath. By late evening, an ominous black cloud had settled over the countryside. The garish red glow in the night sky emblazoned the horizon near the towns of Dayton and Bridgewater.

Was every home aflame? Each barn? Every outbuilding?

Though familiar with The Burning, she hadn't fully comprehended the enormous impact it had on the land. Modern environmentalists would have a fit, as would anyone who loved the earth. Seeing the apocalyptic horror unfold before her was indescribable. But she would try to relate events in tonight's journal entry. Maybe Grandma G. would see and realize how closely the flames were encroaching.

She turned from the horror beyond the window. "It's as if the whole valley burns."

"If Sheridan has his way, it will," Sam muttered, from where he lay on a bed of blankets.

Hettie knelt at his side, one hand cradling his head as she held a cup of water to his lips. She paled, and her freckles stood out against the whiteness of her skin. "Has God's wrath descended upon us?"

"Don't think that," Sam argued. "More like Satan and all his demons have been unleashed."

The lamplight touched on the confusion in her eyes. "Why would God allow this?"

He shrugged, wincing at the pain in his bandaged shoulder. "Don't ask me. Only the Almighty knows the why of anything."

Evie gazed from one to the other. "All I can tell you is this suffering will pass."

"Yes. We must have faith." Hettie firmed her chin, hope in her eyes. "The Lord will not leave us comfortless. The light shall shine again on our valley."

Sam ran the fingers of his uninjured arm through blondish hair like Jack's. The ends brushed his shoulders in the borrowed white shirt. "That may be, miss. But first we must cross through the shadow, and it's a long one."

Hettie exuded determination. "We will get through."

Her 'we shall overcome' spirit inspired Evie. "You are right. We must set aside the differences tearing us apart and work together for good."

Slight tremors ran through Sam. "Maybe so. But I'm tired of this bloody war. Time I went home, to what's left of it. See Mama and my sisters." He lay his head back on the blankets.

The poor guy was worn out and his eyes were a little glassy. Getting him up here hadn't been easy, and further taxed him.

"When you're stronger, you can go," Evie agreed.

Hettie bent near and tucked the cover more snugly around her patient. "Rest now, and mend."

"Thank you, miss. You are most kind." His husky voice was a whisper.

The gentle healer had bathed his arm with herbal water and dabbed more yarrow root over the wound before the bullet was removed, then she'd bandaged him. Not neglecting his sprained ankle, she had applied an herbal poultice of comfrey leaves and wrapped it. He was fortunate to be in her care, and it wasn't lost on Evie that her friend seemed intrigued by this wounded warrior.

She ran her gaze over the accommodations. The wall slanted on one side of them, and he lay in this angular space. Where the narrow room leveled out, ropes of onions and dried herbs hung from the beams overhead in a fragrant contrast to the smoke.

The hideaway housed only a handful of people, and it was cold. She hugged her cloak, as did Hettie. But the attic had provided much-needed sanctuary for many men these past months. Sam was the first avowed Rebel. Others sought to escape conscription in the Confederate Army.

Soon, all of this would be behind the residents of this decimated valley. Rebuilding, replanting, and restocking their burned-out farms would require every scrap of resilience. Many would leave in wagons and never come back. Others would return in the spring.

A pang ran through her at the realization that she and Jack would not be a part of the restoration. Grandma G. had said to watch for the warble phenomenon that acted as a portal to the future, and she was. But leaving the family who had become dear to her, and this era, despite its harshness, would be more wrenching than she'd expected.

Footfalls below them disrupted her thoughts. The footsteps entered her room, and the door to the attic lay behind the dresser along the back wall. They had pushed the heavy furnishing aside to get Sam up here.

Was it Mary, coming to summon the girls from this hidey hole and restore the dresser? Hettie had asked to tend Sam a while longer before going to bed, and Evie wanted to stay with them both. Mary had agreed but was uneasy about his presence.

'Mister Hobbs must not be found in this house,' she had asserted. "It will not bode well for him as a Rebel, or us for concealing him.'

Evie had argued the bluecoats wouldn't come in the dark, and it made no difference if the dresser were out of place, but things were different today. The angry hive had erupted in a frenzy, as if struck with a stick. Maybe they would.

What a terrible predicament if the soldiers came now.

Sam stirred wearily. "That had better be Jack we hear below. Dunham's probably hightailed it back to the pack."

Had Jack returned alone? Was this him?

Hinges creaked and the door to the attic opened. Footfalls sounded on the narrow stairs leading to the secret space where she and her companions waited in tense silence.

The attic had no door, but an opening in the shape of one. A bareheaded figure appeared in the entryway. She looked closely.

Thank God. Jack ducked his head and came through.

What would she have done if a threat had come in his place? They had nowhere to hide. This was it.

He lowered himself on his haunches by her, circling a welcome arm around her shoulders. His clothes were cool from the night air and his skin reddened from riding in the chill breeze. His wind-blown hair framed his handsome face, shadowed in the lamplight. She'd never tire of looking at him, but his demeanor was undeniably grim.

She was instantly alert. "What's wrong?"

"Plenty." His forbidding gaze sought his cousin. "Do you know anything about the death of Union Lieutenant John Meigs? He was felled last evening."

Sam rubbed a chin roughened from days in the saddle, and surveyed Jack with hazel eyes of a similar greenish brown hue. But his expression was mild. "No. I don't inquire the name of every Yankee we fire at. Why?"

"This one was special. Meigs was a favorite of Sheridan's. The general has gone into a rage over his death."

Oh. No. Evie sucked in her breath.

Sam pursed his lips, then asked, "More than usual?"

"A heap more." Jack frowned. "Sheridan ordered his men to burn every building on every farm within three—or was it five—miles of the town of Dayton, plus the entire town. It seems Meigs was shot near there."

"Whereabouts?" Sam asked.

"Along the Swift Run Gap Road."

"Dunham and I weren't there last night."

"He says the same," Jack agreed. "But one of the Rebels in the incident was wounded, which roused my suspicion."

Sam drew his brows together. "There are a lot of wounded Rebs in the valley, Cousin."

"Yes, but your injury is fresh. Then Dunham and I learned the men involved weren't guerillas or bushwhackers, as Sheridan thinks. They are said to be Confederate scouts from Wickham's brigade. The word is that Lieutenant Meigs was shot in a fair fight, not murdered."

"A fine line in war," Sam interjected.

"One we should take care not to cross," Jack flung back, and threw his hands up. "It makes no difference, anyway. Sheridan has doubled his efforts at burning, and the area he's targeting is heavily settled by Mennonites and Brethren families. Pacifists with Unionist sympathies."

Evie was aware of this dark valley history, and yet, to see it playing out was appalling. "The height of cruel irony, and so unfair."

"Tell that to Sheridan," Jack said bitterly. "His burning parties had a busy day."

Hettie roused from her stunned silence. "When will they come here?"

"Tomorrow or the day after at the pace they're going. We are outside the burn range for homes."

"Just," Sam broke in. "You think the men are

measuring, Jack?"

"I expect it depends on the officer in charge of each party and whether he cares to control them."

"That's impossible to know," Evie reasoned. "What about Dayton?"

Jack relaxed slightly. "A sympathetic Union officer by the name of Wildes is pleading with Sheridan to spare the town. Wildes says the townsfolk have been kind to him and his men, and his Brigade, which includes men from West Virginia and Ohio, are loath to carry out Sheridan's orders. Not all Yankees are monsters."

"I never said they were," she contended. "But far too many are eager to apply the torch, as you well know."

"Too well. Question is, what are we to do?"

"Keep out of sight. You cannot fight them when they come. This is not our way." Hettie's quiet voice was firm.

Evie sighed. "I suspect it may be mine."

A hoarse laugh escaped Sam. "It sure as heck is mine. But here I lie. If they torch this house, where does that leave me? Going out the window? Won't do my ankle a power of good."

"Listen." Jack gestured like a coach urging his players to huddle in. "You are in no shape to ride, and the countryside is overrun with the Boys in Blue. I will watch their movements and try to get you to the woods."

"You know what will happen if we're caught. I reckon Sheridan's in a hanging mood." Sam had a fatalistic air.

Jack fingered his stubbled chin. "Yeah. I expect he

is. You might be better off taking your chances up here."

For all Evie's talk of putting differences aside and working together, she was prepared to defend them all. But that wasn't what the Wengers wanted.

How could she explain to them this was her home, too?

She couldn't, unless she revealed her true origins.

Announcing 'I'm from the future,' and references to past lives likely wouldn't go over well. She'd have to wing it on a prayer, and hope Grandma G. was getting her notes.

"Where did you leave Dunham?" Sam finally asked.

"In the kitchen with Mary and the girls." Jack was matter of fact.

"Huh?" Sam grunted. "I figured he would join up with the boys."

"Naw. Mary's cooking corn mush and ham. There's scant food to be had in the camps. Evie has more." Jack slanted his gaze at her carpet bag, peeking from beneath her pile of clothes. "What have you got left?"

"Dried fruit, the chocolate isn't gone yet, and there are cookies. Oh, and I could make us some more coffee."

"If you would, please, Mrs. Ramsey—I mean, Evie—and bring me up a cup with milk and sugar," Sam pleaded. "Just the thing to ward off this chill."

It nagged at her that his eyes looked a bit feverish. "I will. And you can have more of those pills. That should help."

Hettie laid her palm on his forehead. "You are a

little warm. I will bath your brow with herbal water."

"Much obliged, miss."

Jack smiled at him. "I would say you are in good hands."

"A shame I had to get myself shot to have these lovely ladies fussing over me."

It was an enormous pity any of these misfortunes had taken place, but Evie found herself planning an impromptu picnic, and looking forward to it. She might never share this time with these people again, and was determined to savor the moment, despite the destruction descending around them.

Chapter Eighteen

Smoke burned Jack's eyes. A stiff drink would feel good going down his scratchy throat. Nothing would ease the ache in his chest, though, except getting out of the smoke. Impossible. It only thickened. After securing the horses in the sink hole, he stood at the edge of the woods and surveyed the inferno spreading before him. The familiar landscape was ablaze as far as he could see, but the evil cloud obscured his view. The tireless invaders carried out their work like scurrying ants.

Evie slipped from the hazy trees and joined him in the nightmarish reality. The poor girl suffered equally, and he couldn't aid her. Damn it all.

Arms wrapping each other, they looked on in dismay. She shuddered against him as the whistle pierced the ash-laden fog and the successive cracks of rifles felled the animals. The shrill piping and the gun volleys alerted him to the men's whereabouts.

Soon, this menace would be on the Wenger's doorstep. And they had implored Jack to do—nothing. He never felt more helpless. Give him action, not this thumb-twiddling wait while everything around him turned to cinders.

Muffling her mouth and nose with her green cloak, Evie choked out, "It's worse than I could have imagined. Nothing prepares you for this."

"No." And he had seen far too much already.

She lifted reddened eyes to his. "You're resolved to stay, aren't you?"

"I cannot leave you and Sam. The only possible route out of here is to ride west toward the mountains and hope to keep ahead of the blue horde."

Pain welled in her gaze. "Nothing in me wants you to go, but you know every track and cow path. You have a chance, Jack. You might get away."

"As I hope Dunham will do." Their friend rode off at first light with corncakes in his haversack. "But Sam needs the care Hettie gives him to recover. Too often, I have seen men succumb to fever after injury. More soldiers perish from disease and infection than die in battle."

"She will pull him through this," Evie insisted.

Doubt needled Jack. Sam had worsened overnight. "I pray so. He's like a brother to me."

"I know." She squeezed his hand. "You never would have shot him, even when he was hot on your tail."

"Never. Though he often angered me and felled one of the guides." He frowned at the memory.

"War should be outlawed," she said, mopping her eyes with a handkerchief.

He turned his head toward her. "Hasn't it been, in the age you come from?"

"Not remotely. There has to be a better way."

"Indeed." He nodded at the farm house below them hazed by the encroaching smoke. "The Wengers say there is."

"The Mennonites say the same in the future."

"Maybe they're right," he suggested.

"Maybe… It's so hard to resist the urge to fight. I

want to ride at the soldiers with an upraised sword."

"What a splendid sight you would be, sweetheart. An avenging angel. But they would shoot you off your horse."

"There is that." Blinking at tears, she eyed him as if she might never see him again. "You are going to the attic, aren't you?"

"I fear so. I will remain with Sam."

"I think this is where you die, Jack."

He exhaled heavily. "I thought you were going to save me?"

"I am," she said.

"Then save us both. I'm out of ideas." Choking on smoke and emotion, he took her arm. "Let's go. The haze conceals us, and the bluecoats will soon be on our farm."

"*Ours*?" she pressed, coughing into the handkerchief.

"Yes. We began here. Our cabin is at the heart of this house."

She smiled through her tears. "Did we conceal a secret passage in it?"

"If we had, do you not think we would remember?" He hastened her down the hillside through the noxious vapor masquerading as fog.

"There is one, though," she asserted. "The warble."

"We didn't put that there. It's a pathway I cannot begin to understand."

"But it exists. Please, Jack. If I see it, grab Sam and come through with me."

"What do you mean? You speak as if you will be with us?"

"I will. I'm staying in the attic, too." Her tone held

steely resolve.

He opened his mouth in protest, coughing as he argued. "No. Absolutely not."

"If I remain in the yard, I will rage at the men."

"They will ignore or restrain you. I have often seen them dismiss frantic women."

"Exactly," she agreed, to his surprise. "And I will not be able to get to you."

He considered her. "Must you?"

"I'm your guide. There's no hope for us here. The only escape lies in a way out we cannot yet see. The warble is it."

"And if it doesn't come?" he challenged.

"It must. Your and Sam's voice are the Whispers I heard. You called me here. I know that now." Conviction weighed every ragged word.

She baffled him. "The bluecoats may not set the house on fire. We are beyond the burn zone," he reasoned.

"They will. And I will get us out."

Either she was utterly delusional or truly inspired. "How? If the dresser is pushed against the door?"

"That I do not yet know," she conceded. "But we cannot risk you and Sam being found, if men search the house."

He panted in the foul air. "I fear Hettie will try and save us."

"I fear she will insist on remaining by our side. She's fast falling in love with Sam," Evie pointed out.

"Is she, really?" How had Jack not noticed? "God save us all."

Chapter Nineteen

Where are they? Evie knelt at the attic window, searching for sight of the dreaded blue-clad figures pounding up the gray drive. She strained to hear the oncoming beat of hooves, a prayer for Divine mercy repeating in her soul.

She felt uncomfortably like a prisoner awaiting execution but there was a distinct difference between her and a helpless victim about to ascend the scaffold. She had chosen to remain in the attic with Jack and Sam, *insisted* on it. Not because she had a death wish, but to help them escape.

Haze rolled from neighboring farms like fog covering the sea. Orange-red flames shot from burning buildings, and fire devoured hay and wheat shocks still standing in the fields. A blackened pall hung over everything, Hell come to earth.

This heinous mode of warfare was referred to as *scorched earth*. The term hadn't meant much to her in high school, but she totally understood now. It was royally screwed up.

Oh, the arrogance of men! To assume food would always be there no matter how much they wasted, that the earth would remain the same despite the pollution unleashed on it.

Much of the Wengers' hay and corn crop had been harvested, and Jack had helped Paul haul a generous supply to the woods, but the barn wasn't emptied. Removing all the fodder was impossible, nor would it keep out in the weather. The family had planted extra this spring, and this year's harvest was the best in memory. Hopes of expanding their livestock or selling the added bounty had vanished. They would be fortunate to feed their remaining animals through the winter.

Evie's watering eyes masked the barely contained urge to sob uncontrollably. Being stuck up here with the fiery assault almost at their door was harder than she could possibly have imagined. Having faith that a way out would present itself was a stupendous leap, like stepping off a ledge into the abyss and trusting an unseen support awaited her.

'Hold on,' she told herself, fighting the hysteria that threatened to dissolve her into a quivering blob. Even if remaining here had been an ill-fated decision, she wouldn't change it. The three of them must survive or fall together.

She turned toward Jack who knelt behind her by Sam, holding a cold cloth to his forehead. "How's he doing?"

"The same." He dipped the linen in the basin of water, wrung out the excess liquid, and placed the folded cloth on Sam's brow.

Jack's taut expression, his lips pressed together in a hard line, must be how he'd marched into battle at Gettysburg. Unflinching resolve had gotten him this far in a harsh war. Beneath his stern expression, did he battle the emotion threatening to tear her apart?

She studied Sam. Despite the willow bark tea Hettie had administered, his temperature had risen, and it was the herbal version of aspirin. His pale face, glassy eyes, and listlessness told the tale. There was no sign of infection in his wound, but something was wrong. He'd reached a critical juncture in his illness. The fever must break soon, or it would carry him off.

Seeing Jack bent beside the man who was like a brother to him, with nothing to do but sponge his forehead, was exceedingly difficult to watch. She was used to having a well-equipped hospital in town and an ambulance a phone call away. How futile his action seemed.

"Jack," she summoned, keeping her voice down. "Medicine is highly advanced in the future. We better take him with us when we go."

His dozing cousin didn't ask what she was talking about, but Jack regarded her with bemusement in his reddened eyes. "If the pathway appears. Better pray for a miracle."

"I am. Ceaselessly." She froze at the approach of hooves. "Oh, God. They're here." Clapping a hand to her mouth, she pivoted toward the window.

"How many men do you see?" He spoke calmly while she shook, and her heart beat as if a fish thrashed inside it.

The haze obscured her sight as she rapidly counted the mounted figures speeding by in the whiteness like ghosts. "About a dozen bluecoats are riding up the lane."

"A significant party. I was hoping for less."

She swallowed hard. "I was hoping for none but figured that wasn't likely."

"No." His voice was flat. "I pray Hettie refrains from interfering."

Sam grunted in agreement at her name. Fluttering his eyes, he struggled to sit. "She mustn't. Those bastards will shove her to the ground. Backhand her."

Jack restrained him. "Only the worst of the men are rough. Her mother and sisters are with her."

"What can they do?" Coughing from the smoke and whatever else afflicted him, Sam grasped his arm. "I wish we were out there with our rifles like before. Remember those shots we made?" A smile creased his dry lips.

"I will never forget, for the rest of..." Jack neglected to add, 'my life.' Considering that might only be the next twenty minutes, Evie assumed he chose not to bother.

Hettie had begged to stay in the attic with them, and Mary wisely refused. The matriarch had ushered her daughters downstairs to await the inevitable arrival of the soldiers. 'We will plead with the men for Christian charity,' the devout woman had assured Evie and Jack. He gave a nod and Evie had summoned a faint smile, both knowing her efforts would do no good. With rare exceptions, these soldiers were immune to pleas, their humanity extinguished by the war.

Evie glued her eyes on the riders until they disappeared. The instant they were out of sight, she scurried to the window on the other side of her hideaway. "They are in the barn yard, and dismounting," she said breathlessly. "They're wasting no time. Three are coming toward the house." If the sun shone, it would glint off the hardware on their rifles, but the light was eclipsed by haze.

"Oh no," she gasped. "Hettie ran down the steps and into the yard."

"What's happening to her?" Sam asked hoarsely.

"She's dropped on her knees, with her hands upraised, while she entreats them."

Jack gave a low whistle. "Courageous girl."

Sam struggled to rise, with Jack preventing him. "Have they hurt her?"

"No. Just shook their heads, laughed, and passed her by. Then—" Evie broke off as male voices sounded downstairs.

The exchange was muffled to the three anxiously waiting in the attic. But the female outcry was unmistakable, increasing in volume, and there were scuffling sounds. Was furniture being dragged, or worse?

She swiveled her head at Jack, eyeing him in alarm. "Dear God. Do they abuse women?"

"Not in the manner you mean. Sheridan wouldn't allow it."

Sam thrashed in his grip. "I don't trust him to know their actions. You go and put a stop to it, Jack."

"If I thought the girls were suffering abuse I would shove the dresser aside, force open the door, and descend in a fury. I still have my pistol."

He had hidden his and Sam's carbines in the woods.

More cries reached them from the female cluster. "Then what's going on with the girls?" Evie hissed.

"Not that," Jack insisted. "They are probably pleading for their farm."

She darted her gaze at the window as a blue-clad figure charged down the front steps. "One man is heading to the barn with a flaming stick of kindling."

"Sounds about right," Sam muttered.

Sick with horror, she said, "It's been lit."

Smoke curled from the doorway and rose around the great timbered structure she regarded as a sort of earthy cathedral. Orange flames shot through the slats beneath the eves, feeding on hay, chaff, and abundant wood. The ominous crackle reached them in the attic. But the winds were calm. The house wasn't in danger from the barn.

"Another man is torching the chicken coop," she sadly reported. "And the smokehouse."

Jack snorted in disgust. "When you think how long these structures take to build, and how little they further the war effort, it's monstrous to destroy them."

The washhouse was next, but she said nothing. Her companions knew every building would be lit. Thankfully, Sam's clothes had been cleaned and restored to him before they were spotted by inquiring eyes.

Smoke billowed in the yard, and dismay flooded Evie. The house was an island in a sea of smoke. If only Mary had let Jack fire warning shots at the burners. He might have frightened them off. Fear of escalating violence had prevented her from agreeing to any defense, and maybe she was right. He was only one against a dozen or more.

Cries sharpened downstairs. Was the remaining man threatening to set the house on fire?

Every girl set up a lament that would have moved all but the flintiest hearts. The family didn't dare plead for the lives upstairs, or Jack and Sam would be taken and imprisoned or executed. And Sam would never survive. But they entreated their tormenters for the mercy they did not possess.

She exchanged glances with Jack, trying to still his cousin. They could but pray the soldiers rode off before the fire was beyond the families' ability to extinguish. Hysteria engulfed the downstairs. Guttural shouts resounded from the men. Footfalls creaked on the steps and in the hall.

Were soldiers searching the house? Were they looting what little the family had, or were the sisters claiming a few last-minute articles?

Tumult beyond the window drew Evie's focus. Converging bluecoats hauled Mary and the girls down the front steps, and away from the house. In their arms, the forlorn sisters carried some bedding. The largest girl hugged the big family Bible. No one cried harder than Hettie, reaching her arms to the attic, though to the men it would appear she reached for her home.

"You cannot!" she shrieked.

But they could.

There were no words for the anguish inside Evie. She looked at Jack. This was it.

The alleluia moment when angels appeared had better transpire soon. In seconds, a choking cloud would roll upstairs and into their hiding space. Smoke surging ahead of the flames would get them. And it would happen very fast.

What she sought, she couldn't say, but would know when she found it. Circling her numb gaze at the attic, she took in the bunches of herbs, the braided onions, her pile of clothing and the carpet bag. A single trunk, the low stool with an unlit candle, a plate and cups, the blankets on the floor.. little else. These simple, sparse furnishing comprised the décor.

After what seemed forever, but was only a

moment, an alternate reality floated into her vision. She glimpsed the jumble accumulated over the years by people with a lot more 'stuff' to collect. This hadn't been here before and didn't belong to the Wengers.

God in heaven, *the warble* had arrived. Her angel moment. A halleluiah choir should accompany it.

She waved her hand at what she trusted wasn't a mirage. "Jack do you see?" She forced the hoarse question from her burning throat.

He stared where she gestured with reddened eyes. As he did so, the phenomenon disappeared, and he turned his disbelieving gaze at her. "What?"

"The warble was there a second ago. Fading in and out. We've got to take Sam down the attic stairs to my room. It will come again. Stronger, the next time, I pray."

"If we go down there and open the door to your chamber and you are wrong, the smoke will get to us that much sooner. We will forfeit any chance we might have."

"I know. But every instinct urges me on. It's now, Jack."

Fatalism in his gaze, he nodded. He had resigned himself to his fate. But this was their salvation.

Sam twisted in his grip. "What is she going on about? Not that it much matters. We're as good as dead."

"No. We are getting out of here, Cousin. Let's go." Jack unfolded the wet linen and tied it around Sam's nose and mouth.

Evie wet her handkerchief and bound it around her face below her eyes. Jack did the same with his kerchief and heaved the ill and injured man to his feet. Sam sagged in his arms. Evie lent her aid. Sam could barely stand. Together, they helped him across the attic floor, her skirts trailing behind, and paused at the opening.

"I'll go first." Jack turned and descended the steps backward, bracing Sam between them.

She followed, crippled by her skirts. Wrenching the lengths up with one hand, she helped Sam with the other. But the lethal vapor traveled up the narrow steps.

How would she see the warble in this murky mist, coughing her head off? The three of them choked, gasping for air. They would succumb to the smoke before they took another step.

Jack paused before her bedroom door in the tight space between it and the stairs leading to the attic. There wasn't room for three of them and she waited behind him and Sam on the steps. He hesitated. The door formed their only barrier.

He gestured for silence, and they tried unsuccessfully to stifle coughs. A loud grating of wood across the floor sounded on the other side of the door, the dresser being moved. Then a hand turned the knob.

Whose?

Soldiers? She couldn't see who it was.

The door wrenched open and he reached for his pistol.

"Come on. Quickly," a woman rapped.

"Wait, Jack." Evie knew that voice. Recognition washed her with hope.

Chapter Twenty

Despite Evie's assurance of coming help, Jack surveyed their rescuer as if she had sailed from the moon. The plump middle-aged woman wore a lavender gown, silver hair mounded on her head, and a white mask covering her nose and mouth. Reaching out an able arm, she snagged Sam and helped Jack get him through the door into Evie's room. The poor girl tumbled after them. He steadied her before she fell in a heap.

As she straightened, a phenomenon occurred, as miraculous as if they were shielded by angels' wings. He and the others were enveloped in what must be Evie's warble, like the eye of a storm. Beyond this clear circle was the odious cloud, while inside the air was clean and herb-scented, and the furnishings different than those he'd known before. The Wengers never owned this opulent carpet in rich shades of purple and gold.

They didn't have a brass lamp with an ornamental white shade on the stand beside a four-poster bed. Their bed and comforter were plain. No colorful guilt spread over the mattress. If they'd had these possessions, they would have been stolen from them by Rebels or the looting bluecoats.

They pulled the cloths from their faces in wonder and crumpled the linen in their hands.

"What in the name of Sam Hill is this?" Sam croaked. "Have we entered heaven, with a view of Hell?"

"You are in between times," the woman explained, stuffing a sealed envelope into his coat pocket. "Take one of the enclosed pills morning and evening, and you will be well."

"Are you an angel?" He voiced Jack's query.

Blue eyes the same hue as Evie's sparkled above her mask. "Near enough. I'm this young lady's grandmother."

Realization dawned. Here stood the benevolent being he had heard so much about.

Evie squeezed his arm. "Grandma G. this is my Jack, and his cousin, Sam."

The tidings seemed to come as no surprise to the woman. "I've been expecting you. We have work to do. Come on." She picked up an unfamiliar instrument he hadn't noticed—a foreign rifle, or cannon, perhaps— and charged ahead.

They stepped behind her through the wavering bubble. He and Evie followed, supporting Sam between them. The hateful miasma enclosed the trio, and wrenching coughs returned.

Their dogged commander charged down the foggy staircase in a swirl of lavender. They were hard-pressed to keep pace with her and arrived, choking, at the bottom of the steps to see her blast the inferno billowing from the horsehair couch. This must be where the fire had begun with a stick of tossed kindling. Typical of the soldiers. She doused a nearby chair catching fire and smothered orange tendrils climbing the wall.

How on earth did she do it? He had never seen a fire put out with white foam before, nor had Sam. Or anybody.

Her task completed, she tore outdoors, yelling, "Get away from here!" And put the weapon to a second good use. "Let these people go and leave now!" She turned the frothy deluge on the soldiers keeping the distraught family at bay while their home burned. Or so they thought.

The men lurched back at the arrival of this seemingly insane woman wielding an alien weapon. She covered the scrambling Yankees with the white spray. No need to repeat her order. Fearful for their lives, they bolted for their horses and galloped away. Comical to see, if they hadn't left such devastation behind.

She scanned the result of their deeds with narrow eyes. Jack knew that look. Pure rage. Then the anger in her expression faded and she turned to the stunned family.

Circling an arm around Mary, she explained. "I am Mrs. McIntyre, Evie's grandmother. I've come to take her and Jack home with me."

Had she truly? He was leaving? Too flabbergasted for speech, he stood with Evie, and upheld Sam.

The woman she called Grandma G. tapped the unlikely weapon. "This is a fire extinguisher, not normally used for battle. The soldiers will recover. I'm sorry the outbuildings are too far gone for me to save, but your house is spared."

"*Denki*," Mary offered with trembling lips, between the coughs tearing from her chest. "We feared all lost, and these dear souls perished." She gestured at

Jack. "Like a son to me." She could not continue. Emotions were too great, as was the noxious vapor.

He nodded at her, and she blurred before his brimming eyes.

"I understand." Their rescuer turned from Mary to Hettie, her dumbfounded expression a reflection of his incredulity. "Take care of Sam, dear girl. I left him some healing tablets. See he takes one morning and evening until they're gone. He will be all right."

"Thank you. You are an angel sent from heaven above." Praising their rescuer, Hettie sprang forward. She closed strong arms around Sam, and Jack relinquished his grip. Fixing her astonished gaze on Mrs. McIntyre, she asked, "How did you make it past the soldiers to gain entrance to the house?"

Mystery cloaked the newcomer's eyes. "I know another way."

"The back?" Hettie faltered.

"Another route besides that."

"But there is none," the girl persisted.

"There is. One day you may discover it. Thank you for looking after my granddaughter. We three must go now." She nudged Evie and Jack. "Say your goodbyes."

He didn't know where to begin. How was he to part from these dear people? Was he leaving forever? Did he have a choice? Questions tumbled in his dizzied senses.

He shot a last look around. The barn shuddered and hissed in the greedy flames consuming the once comforting shelter. Outbuildings crackled, and he could see little of the loved farmstead through the blackened smoke. The familiar faces around him were a mix of wonder and grief.

Stumbling through the motions, he embraced Sam. "Take care of yourself and Buck." Pain knifed him at the thought of leaving them both.

His cousin closed a weak arm around him. "I will keep him safe for your return."

"Sam," he said huskily in his ear. "I'm not sure I am coming back."

He tightened his embrace as much as a sick man could. "I'll miss you, Jack," he choked out.

"Yeah. Me, too. There's food and fodder at my cabin, remember." He turned to Mary, tears streaking her lined cheeks. "I would stay if I could."

She flung her arms around his neck in an unusually demonstrative embrace. "*Gott segen eich.*"

"God bless you," he answered in turn, enfolding the petite figure. "You have been like a mother. Say goodbye to Paul for me." He detached himself from her and lifted a shaky hand to the weeping girls. "*Gott segen eich.*"

Their world had turned on its head, and here he was leaving them. Why now?

He only knew his rescuer was insistent and an inner voice nudged him to do as she decreed.

Hettie pressed a kiss to his cheek. "Have care, Jack, wherever life takes you."

Weeping so hard, she could scarcely see, let alone talk, Evie hugged her friend. "I will miss you more than I can say," she gulped out, mopping her face with the handkerchief. She bade a tearful farewell to Mary and the huddled family. "I wish I could help you rebuild."

Hettie clasped her hands. "Return to us, if you can."

"I will." A sob broke into her reply.

Mrs. McIntyre gripped her granddaughter and Jack by the arm. "Farewell all. Our time here wanes."

The exchange lasted only moments. The bewildered group stared after them as she hustled the reluctant couple back indoors. Battling for breath in the lingering smoke, they dashed up the cloudy stairs and into Evie's room. The chamber appeared as it had in the Wengers' care. Shouldn't it be altered?

"Go into the closet. The warble is strongest in that spot now," their guide directed. She turned the knob, half-pushing them through, and followed behind.

At first, Jack was only aware of Evie's sweet warmth beside him in the darkness. The tight space was as he recalled, but the next moment, everything had changed. They stepped into a different place. The choking vapor and every vestige of the fire had gone.

Evie pulled a string dangling in the gloom and light flooded the compact room. Was it the closet she had spoken of?

Boxes made of a material resembling brown paper filled the space, leaving scant floor for them to stand, and he ducked his head.

What in the world? He slanted his still watering eyes at a statue that bore a strong resemblance to Santa Claus. Did he really see reindeer figures beside the jolly old elf?

He sniffed spiced cider. "Am I mad?"

"No. You are not losing your mind." The matriarch took the mask from her face and set the extinguisher down. "You are home now."

She opened the door and ushered them into Evie's chamber. This room resembled the one he had glimpsed before, only it was fully corporeal and smokeless now.

Unsure what might come or go next, he wrapped his arm around Evie. Whatever transpired, they would face it together.

She appeared as dazed as he felt. "How did you know to arrive when you did, Grandma G.?"

"Your journal entries, dear girl. The last one read, 'They're coming,' and you gave the hour."

"So I did. Not that long ago, either."

"Actually, it was over one hundred and fifty years ago," Mrs. McIntyre amended, to Jack's utter disbelief.

"This is too much to take in," Evie murmured.

He couldn't begin to absorb it all.

She surveyed her room. "Everything is just as I left it."

Was it? He stared around him at the finely furnished chamber and gazed out the window.

Beyond the house were blue skies and green leaves rustling in branching trees, taller than the ones he recalled. Where fire had left ruin, fields of lavender now thrived. Nearer to the house, spread a garden filled with herbs and flowers. Here and there, visitors stopped to admire a bloom.

Best of all, horses kicked up their heels in the verdant meadow. What magnificent animals, surrounded by beauty. If a trumpet had sounded, he could scarcely be more persuaded he had arrived in heaven. Surely, he must have.

His heart leapt in joy, but guilt nagged him. "This is marvelous, but should we not have remained behind and helped the family?"

The kind woman circled her arm through his and patted it. "Paul will return, and the Wenger sons will come home from the north with bags of grain and tools to help rebuild. You got the boys out of the valley, and they will be part of its salvation. You fought your war the best you knew how, Jack."

"We lost," he reminded her.

"Yes, and no. It ended as it must. Your life is here now."

He turned puzzled eyes on her. "How so?"

"You died in the attic that fateful day. Only the house brought you forward when Evie went back for you."

A chill crawled down his neck.

She let him consider this unfathomable assertion for a moment. "You cannot remain in an era you no longer occupy, dear boy, any more than a soldier felled in battle can resume the life he once knew. You will upset the time continuum."

Whatever that was. "Why did we leave Sam behind then?"

"Unbelievable as this may be, your cousin survived. In the original version of your lives, you shielded him with your body, and the family dragged him out before he perished. But the smoke claimed you."

Evie sucked in her breath. "Jack saved Sam? Holy cow." She closed her arms around his chest. "How brave."

He held her to him. "What of his fever? He was ill."

"Hettie eventually prevailed in her cure. He will heal far faster with the medication I left him. When Evie mentioned his illness in her journal, I wasn't certain if he might not be worse than before. You see, it is vital that he survive."

"Why?" they chorused.

"He is Evie's great-great-great-great grandfather. We wouldn't be here if he hadn't lived."

Jack sank onto the bed and gaped at the woman.

Evie lowered herself beside him. "Who did Sam marry?"

"Why Hettie, of course," her grandmother said, as if there could be no other choice. "Jack brought them together."

He tried to envision his reprobate cousin as Evie's forebear, and wed to a devout Mennonite. How could this be?

Her expression mirrored his stupefaction. "I'm best friends with my ancestors? What relation does that make Jack and me?"

"Very distant cousins, so don't worry about it. Sam and Hettie restored his family's homeplace and lived there happily for many years. She was a marvelous influence and calmed him down." Mrs. McIntyre tapped a finger to her creased forehead. "Bizarre to think their lives are lived, while yours have only just begun. You two have a second chance."

"Yes." Jack stared bemusedly at his would-be wife.

"Another thing. You remember Sundown, the young man I recently hired?" the woman continued, with a distracted nod from Evie. "Excellent worker, by the way. He is also a descendent of Sam and Hettie's. Another distant cousin."

Evie groaned. "You knew all this and never said?"

"I didn't know everything," her grandmother clarified. "After you went back, I learned more. It's amazing, really."

"Really," Jack echoed hoarsely.

She grew brisk. "I realize you two are overwhelmed, and in need of a nice hot shower to wash off the smoke and grime. Evie will explain about showers, and I have some clothes for you, Jack. Then meet me in the kitchen for hot coffee, biscuits, and jam. We have much to discuss."

Her words washed over him. "Where do I stay?"

"With Evie, of course. You are her husband."

"But we did not wed properly."

"You did once. We will observe another ceremony. Seems we have a wedding to plan."

Evie clasped his hand, entwining their fingers together. "You will remain here with me, won't you?"

"Where else would I go? You are everything."

The matriarch nodded in satisfaction. "Good. That's settled most agreeably. I am leaving you both the farm when I've gone. It was yours to begin with. You took the long way 'round, but you are finally home together."

"Finally," he softly repeated.

Joy stirred in his soul amid the confusion clouding his mind, like the smoke they had left behind.

Tears glistened in Evie's eyes. "You have a lot to get used to, but I will be with you every step of the way."

What more could he ask?

Chapter Twenty-One

One Month Later, Evie and Jack's Wedding Reception

Savoring their magical night, Evie circled in a waltz with her handsome husband. The garden had never looked lovelier; added blooms burst from pots and wicker baskets. Color filled every nook. And Jack was splendid. Regal, even.

He was the definition of masculine appeal in a black dress-coat with a full collar, a vest of the same rich fabric, and matching doeskin pants that enhanced his tall, lean build. Black leather shoes had replaced his customary boots and he'd drawn on white gloves rather than the brown pair he used for riding. Trim blond hair curled at his ears and the nape of his neck. He was the perfect Victorian gentleman, and wore elegance with an easy charm.

Prince Albert had nothing on Jack. If a cowboy could be a prince, he pulled off the look. No one acquainted with the rugged man of his former life would guess this was the same scout who had ridden throughout the valley, both rescuing men and fighting them, depending on the circumstances.

Only very occasionally, when annoyed, the steel that crossed Jack's gaze reminded her of the officer they had left behind. That man still lurked inside him.

He commanded respect.

Evie trusted she complemented him in a simple yet elegant ivory satin gown. The flowing dress had a lacy neckline and full skirt buoyed with layers of petticoats. Flower motifs edged her delicate lace veil, and a circlet of lavender crowned her head. The scent wafted from her and trailed on the light breeze. Roses also lent their perfume.

Tea lights floated in bowls filled with lavender tinted water. The hue washed through table cloths, flower arrangements, seat cushions, tiny mints, and punch. This home wasn't called Lavender House for nothing.

Proud and smiling, Grandma G. resided over the evening like a queen. Pictures of the grand affair would find their way into brochures and onto the farm's website, Evie suspected. And why not? Her grandmother had taken an enormous risk to help them escape a fiery death.

As she and Jack circled beneath strings of white lights, she pondered their miraculous wedding, and smiled at her mother and father dancing nearby. Her younger sister and two brothers, parked at the refreshment table, eyed her with affection and an expression she never thought to see, respect.

They wound past Sundown. To her surprise, his intent gaze was fixed on her. She glimpsed yearning in his eyes before he caught himself and glanced away.

She'd had no idea he felt like this. Her conscience pricked her momentarily. But he was a good-looking young man and would find someone, or they would find him, before long.

She tilted her face at Jack, trying to fathom all they

had experienced together. And to think her mind-blowing adventure began because she was afraid of the closet.

Eyes awash with tenderness, he gazed at her. "Is this real?"

"Yes. The beginning of the rest of our lives. We'll get it right this time."

He nodded at her family. "When shall we tell them?"

They were still in ignorance regarding his true origins. Evie had accounted for his unawareness of all things modern by insisting he was passionate about the past.

She shrugged. "Later?" She'd already put it off a month. Sundown, who lived in the house, was bound to have suspicions about her two-week hiatus, plus she'd learned he belonged to a paranormal investigation society.

As it turned out, for most people, all Grandma G. had to say to explain her long absence was, 'Evie's met a guy. She's head over heels.'

After that, the only question the woman had to field was when would the family get to see him? And Jack had gained instant popularity when they did, although they wondered about him. How could they not?

As thrilled and grateful as Evie was to be here with him, part of her wished she could see Mary and Paul, Sam and Hettie again. She knew he felt the same. Like the sun sinking behind the hills, imbuing the sky with rose, streaked saffron-gold, their lives were shot through with joy, mingled with bitter sweetness.

One thing that had brought them both a sense of

peace was the letter she found left for her in the hiding place beneath the floorboards. Hettie had written: *Two years have passed since you and Jack left us so mysteriously. Many times, we have spoken of you both with deep fondness.*

It has taken much hard work, but my brothers have returned, and the barn and outbuildings are restored. You would love to see the lambs at play in the meadow. Calves are born. Polly has a new foal and the chickens enjoy their pen.

Sam and I were wed in the spring and I live in his home in Augusta County now. We are happy together. Do not fear for our family, Evie. God is good. With Love, your friend Hettie.

P.S. Jack forgot his hat.

Evie had smiled at this, but she hadn't tried to leave a reply. Hettie's words were penned long ago, and the ink faded. The messages only worked from the past to the present, not the reverse.

Someday, if the warble returned, and the path allowed, she and Jack might step back through time just for a moment…

Meanwhile, they danced.

Beth Trissel

Author's Notes

My husband and I live on a farm in the Shenandoah Valley that has been in his family for five generations. We are in the area hardest hit by The Burning that took place in the fall of eighteen sixty-four when Union forces under Major General Philip Sheridan brought hard war to the residents of the valley. Mills, barns, crops, supplies, anything of possible value to the Confederate forces, were systematically torched by Union cavalry. Many homes were also burned, particularly around us. Thousands of farm animals were slaughtered in their pens or taken for the army's use. Horses were rounded up.

The valley's pacifist Mennonites and Brethren, most of whom were loyal to the Union, were not spared. My husband's Mennonite ancestors were among them. The Samuel Shank family lost everything they had, except for the family Bible which they managed to save. Older family members retold this story at reunions. Many Mennonites were forced to flee the valley or face a harsh winter.

In his book, *The Burning: Sheridan's Devastation of the Shenandoah Valley*, late valley historian and author John Heatwole, concludes: "The civilian population of the valley was affected to a greater extent than was the populace of any other region during the war, including those in the path of Sherman's infamous march to the sea in Georgia."

In addition to John Heatwole's book, another valuable resource is *Unionists and the Civil War Experience in the Shenandoah Valley*, compiled by David S. Rodes and Norman R. Wenger. A lot of information is given about the Unionist Underground Railroad. Many of the places and people mentioned in these books are not only familiar, but on my doorstep.

My English Scots-Irish ancestors were also in the valley during the Civil War. They were among the first settlers of Augusta County at the southern end. They left fascinating and deeply moving accounts. Their homes remain, having escaped the worst of The Burning.

My great-great-grandfather, George W. Finley, first Lt. of company K in the Fifty-Sixth VA Regiment, was in Pickett's Charge at Gettysburg. He crossed the stone wall at the Angle beside General Armistead, whom he saw fall. After realizing the battle was over, Finley was one of the few surviving officers who surrendered the remnant of his regiment. He spent the next two years incarcerated in seven different Union prisons and is one of the "Immortal 600," the southern officers who were placed under the walls of Ft Morris in Charleston Harbor in retaliation for the mistreatment of Union officers.

Nearly blind and near death, he was saved by a Baltimore woman who nursed him back to health, interceded with General Grant, and got him released in May eighteen sixty-five. He returned home and became a Presbyterian minister after the war. Finley promised God on Cemetery Ridge that he would serve him all his days if he survived, and he kept his vow.

A word about the author…

Married to my high school sweetheart, I live on a farm in the Shenandoah Valley of Virginia with my human family and furbabies. An avid gardener, my love of herbs and heirloom plants figures into my work. The rich history of Virginia, the Native Americans, and the people who journeyed here from far beyond her borders are at the heart of my inspiration. I'm especially drawn to colonial America, the drama of the American Revolution, and the Civil War. In addition to historical romance, I also write time travel, paranormal, YA fantasy romance, and nonfiction.

https://bethtrissel.wordpress.com/

Thank you for purchasing
this publication of The Wild Rose Press, Inc.

For questions or more information
contact us at
info@thewildrosepress.com.

The Wild Rose Press, Inc.
www.thewildrosepress.com

To visit with authors of
The Wild Rose Press, Inc.
join our yahoo loop at
http://groups.yahoo.com/group/thewildrosepress/